I0564611

O. P. (Oscar Penn) Fitzgerald

California Sketches

New Series

O. P. (Oscar Penn) Fitzgerald

California Sketches
New Series

ISBN/EAN: 9783337010904

Printed in Europe, USA, Canada, Australia, Japan

Cover: Foto ©Andreas Hilbeck / pixelio.de

More available books at **www.hansebooks.com**

CALIFORNIA SKETCHES.

NEW SERIES.

BY O. P. FITZGERALD

WITH AN INTRODUCTION BY BISHOP GEORGE F. PIERCE.

The bearded men in rude attire,
With nerves of steel and hearts of fire,
The women few but fair and sweet,
Like shadowy visions dim and fleet,
Again I see, again I hear,
As down the past I dimly peer,
And muse o'er buried joy and pain,
And tread the hills of youth again.

SOUTHERN METHODIST PUBLISHING HOUSE,
NASHVILLE, TENN.
1882.

Entered according to Act of Congress, in the year 1881, by

O. P. FITZGERALD,

in the Office of the Librarian of Congress, at Washington.

A WORD.

ENCORES are usually anticlimaxes. I never did
like them. Yet here I am again before the public
with another book of "CALIFORNIA SKETCHES." The
kind treatment given to the former volume, of which six
editions have been printed and sold; the expressed wishes
of many friends who have said, Give us another book;
and my own impulse, have induced me to venture upon a
second appearance. If much of the song is in the minor
key, it had to be so: these Sketches are from real life, and
"all lives are tragedies." THE AUTHOR.

Nashville, September, 1881.

INTRODUCTION.

THE first issue of the "California Sketches" was very popular, deservedly so. The distinguished Author has prepared a Second Series. In this fact the reading public will rejoice.

In these books we have the romance and *prestige* of fiction; the thrill of incident and adventure; the wonderful phases of society in a new country, and under the pressure of strong and peculiar excitements; human character loose from the restraints of an old civilization—a settled order of things; individuality unwarped by imitation—free, varied, independent. The materials are rich, and they are embodied in a glowing narrative. The writer himself lived amid the scenes and the people he describes, and, as a citizen, a preacher, and an editor, was an important factor among the forces destined to mold the elements which were to be formulated in the politics of the State and the enterprises of the Church. A close observer, gifted with a keen discrimination and retentive memory, a decided relish for the ludicrous and the sportive, and always ready to give a religious turn to thought and conversation, he is admirably adapted to portray and recite what he saw, heard, and felt.

These Sketches furnish good reading for anybody. For the young they are charming, full of entertainment, and not wanting in moral instruction. They will gratify the taste of those who love to read, and, what is more important, beget the appetite for books among the dull and indifferent. He who can stimulate children and young men and women to read renders a signal service to society at large. Mental growth depends much upon reading, and the fertilization of the original soil by the habit wisely directed connects vitally with the outcome and harvest of the future.

Dr. Fitzgerald is doing good service in the work already done, and I trust the patronage of the people will encourage him to give us another and another of the same sort. At my house we all read the "California Sketches"—old and young—and long for more.

G. F. PIERCE.

CONTENTS.

DICK.

DICK was a Californian. We made his acquaintance in Sonora about a month before Christmas, *Anno Domini* 1855. This is the way it happened:

At the request of a number of families, the lady who presided in the curious little parsonage near the church on the hill-side had started a school for little girls. The public schools might do for the boys, but were too mixed for their sisters—so they thought. Boys could rough it—they were a rough set, any way—but the girls must be raised according to the traditions of the old times and the old homes. That was the view taken of the matter then, and from that day to this the average California girl has been superior to the average California boy. The boy gets his bias from the street; the girl, from her mother at home. The boy plunges into the life that surges around him; the girl only feels the touch of its waves as they break upon the embankments of home. The boy gets more of the father; the girl gets more of the mother. This may explain their relative superiority. The school for girls was started on condition that it should be free, the proposed teacher refusing all compensation. That part of the arrangement was a failure, for at the end of the first month every little girl brought a handful of money, and laid it on the teacher's desk. It must have been a concerted matter. That quiet, unselfish woman had suddenly become a money-maker in spite of herself. (Use was found for the coin in the course of events.) The school was opened with a Psalm, a prayer, and a little song in which the sweet voices of the little Jewish, Spanish, German, Irish, and American maidens united heartily. Dear children! they are scattered now. Some of them have died, and some of them have met with what is worse than death. There was one bright Spanish girl, slender, graceful as a willow, with the fresh Castilian blood mantling her cheeks, her bright eyes beaming with mischief and affection. She was a beautiful child, and her winning ways made her a pet in the little school. But surrounded as the bright, beautiful girl was, Satan had a mortgage on her from her birth, and her fate was too dark and sad to be told in these pages. She inherited evil condition, and perhaps evil blood, and her evil life seemed to be inevitable. Poor child of sin, whose very beauty was thy curse, let the curtain fall upon thy fate and name; we leave thee in the hands of the pitying Christ, who hath said, "Where little is given little will be required." Little was given thee in the way of opportunity, for it was a mother's hand that bound thee with the chains of evil.

Among the children that came to that remarkable academy on the hill was little Mary Kinneth, a thin, delicate child, with mild blue eyes, flaxen hair, a peach complexion, and the blue veins on her temples that are so often the sign of delicacy of organization and the presage of early death. Mike Kinneth, her father, was a drinking Irishman, a good-hearted fellow when sober, but pugnacious and disposed to beat his wife when drunk. The poor woman came over to see me one day. She had been crying, and there was an ugly bruise on her cheek.

"Your riverence will excuse me," she said, courtesying, "but I wish you would come over and spake a word to me husband. Mike's a kind, good craythur except when he is dhrinking, but then he is the very Satan himself."

"Did he give you that bruise on your face, Mrs. Kinneth?"

"Yis; he came home last night mad with the whisky, and was breaking ivery thing in the house.

I tried to stop him, and thin he bate me--O! he never did that before!   My heart is broke!"

Here the poor woman broke down and cried, hiding her face in her apron.

"Little Mary was asleep, and she waked up frightened and crying to see her father in such a way.   Seeing the child seemed to sober him a little, and he stumbled on to the bed, and fell asleep. He was always kind to the child, dhrunk or sober. And there is a good heart in him if he will only stay away from the dhrink."

"Would he let me talk to him?"

"Yis; we belong to the old Church, but there is no priest here now, and the kindness your lady has shown to little Mary has softened his heart to ye both.   And I think he feels a little sick and ashamed this mornin', and he will listen to kind words now if iver."

I went to see Mike, and found him half-sick and in a penitent mood.   He called me "Father Fitz- gerald," and treated me with the utmost polite- ness and deference.   I talked to him about little Mary, and his warm Irish heart opened to me at once.

"She is a good child, your riverence, and shame on the father that would hurt or disgrace her!"

The tears stood in Mike's eyes as he spoke the words.

"All the trouble comes from the whisky. Why not give it up?"

"By the help of God I will!" said Mike, grasping my hand with energy.

And he did. I confess that the result of my visit exceeded my hopes. Mike kept away from the saloons, worked steadily, little Mary had no lack of new shoes and neat frocks, and the Kinneth family were happy in a humble way. Mike always seemed glad to see me, and greeted me warmly.

One morning about the last of November there was a knock at the door of the little parsonage. Opening the door, there stood Mrs. Kinneth with a turkey under her arm.

"Christmas will soon be coming, and I've brought ye a turkey for your kindness to little Mary and your good talk to Mike. He has not touched a dhrop since the blissed day ye spake to him. Will ye take the turkey, and my thanks wid it?"

The turkey was politely and smilingly accepted, and Mrs. Kinneth went away looking mightily pleased.

I extemporized a little coop for our turkey. Having but little mechanical ingenuity, it was a difficult job, but it resulted more satisfactorily than did my attempt to make a door for the miniature kitchen attached to the parsonage. My object was to nail some cross-pieces on some plain boards, hang it on hinges, and fasten it on the inside by a leather strap attached to a nail. The model in my mind was, as the reader sees, of the most simple and primitive pattern. I spent all my leisure time for a week at work on that door. I spoiled the lumber, I blistered my hands, I broke several dollars' worth of carpenter's tools, which I had to pay, and—then I hired a man to make that door! This was my last effort in that line of things, excepting the turkey-coop, which was the very last. It lasted four days, at the end of which time it just gave way all over, and caved in. Fortunately, it was no longer needed. Our turkey would not leave us. The parsonage fare suited him, and he staid, and throve, and made friends.

We named him Dick. He is the hero of this Sketch. Dick was intelligent, sociable, and had a good appetite. He would eat any thing, from a crust of bread to the pieces of candy that the school-girls would give him as they passed. He became as gentle as a dog, and would answer to his name. He had the freedom of the town, and went where he pleased, returning at meal-times, and at night to roost on the western end of the kitchen-roof. He would eat from our hands, looking at us with a sort of human expression in his shiny eyes. If he were a hundred yards away, all we had to do was to go to the door and call out, "Dick!"

"Dick!" once or twice, and here he would come, stretching his long legs, and saying, "Oot," "oot," "oot" (is that the way to spell it?). He got to like going about with me. He would go with me to the post-office, to the market, and sometimes he would accompany me in a pastoral visit. Dick was well known and popular. Even the bad boys of the town did not throw stones at him. His ruling passion was the love of eating. He ate between meals. He ate all that was offered to him. Dick was a pampered turkey, and made the most of his good luck and popularity. He was never in low spirits, and never disturbed except when a dog came about him. He disliked dogs, and seemed to distrust them.

The days rolled by, and Dick was fat and happy. It was the day before Christmas. We had asked two bachelors to take Christmas-dinner with us, having room and chairs for just two more persons. (One of our four chairs was called a stool—it had a bottom and three legs, one of which was a little shaky, and no back.) There was a constraint upon us both all day. I knew what was the matter, but said nothing. About four o'clock in the afternoon Dick's mistress sat down by me, and, after a pause, remarked:

"Do you know that to-morrow is Christmas-day?"

"Yes, I know it."

Another pause.   I had nothing to say just then.

"Well, if—if—if any thing is to be done about that turkey, it is time it were done."

"Do you mean Dick?"

"Yes," with a little quiver in her voice.

"I understand you—you mean to kill him— poor Dick! the only pet we ever had."

She broke right down at this, and began to cry.

"What is the matter here?" said our kind, energetic neighbor, Mrs. T——, who came in to pay us one of her informal visits.   She was from Philadelphia, and, though a gifted woman, with a wide range of reading and observation of human life, was not a sentimentalist.   She laughed at the weeping mistress of the parsonage, and, going to the back-door, she called out:

"Dick!" "Dick!"

Dick, who was taking the air high up on the hillside, came at the call, making long strides, and sounding his "Oot," "oot," "oot," which was the formula by which he expressed all his emotions, varying only the tone.

Dick, as he stood with outstretched neck and a look of expectation in his honest eyes, was scooped up by our neighbor, and carried off down the hill in the most summary manner.

In about an hour Dick was brought back.   He was dressed.   He was also stuffed.

THE DIGGERS.

THE Digger Indian holds a low place in the scale of humanity. He is not intelligent; he is not handsome; he is not very brave. He stands near the foot of his class, and I fear he is not likely to go up any higher. It is more likely that the places that know him now will soon know him no more, for the reason that he seems readier to adopt the bad white man's whisky and diseases than the good white man's morals and religion. Ethnologically he has given rise to much conflicting speculation, with which I will not trouble the gentle reader. He has been in California a long time, and he does not know that he was ever anywhere else. His pedigree does not trouble him; he is more concerned about getting something to eat. It is not because he is an agriculturist that he is called a Digger, but because he grabbles for wild roots, and has a general fondness for dirt. I said he was not handsome, and when we consider his rusty, dark-brown

(15)

color, his heavy features, fishy black eyes, coarse
black hair, and clumsy gait, nobody will dispute
the statement. But one Digger is uglier than another, and an old squaw caps the climax.

The first Digger I ever saw was the best-look-
ing. He had picked up a little English, and loafed
around the mining-camps picking up a meal where
he could get it. He called himself "Captain
Charley," and, like a true native American, was
proud of his title. If it was self-assumed, he was
still following the precedent set by a vast host of
captains, majors, colonels, and generals, who never
wore a uniform or hurt anybody. He made his
appearance at the little parsonage on the hill-side
in Sonora one day, and, thrusting his bare head
into the door, he said :

"Me Cappin Charley," tapping his chest com-
placently as he spoke.

Returning his salutation, I waited for him to
speak again.

"You got grub—coche carne?" he asked, mix-
ing his Spanish and English.

Some food was given him, which he snatched
rather eagerly, and began to eat at once. It was
evident that Captain Charley had not breakfasted
that morning. He was a hungry Indian, and when
he got through his meal there was no reserve of
rations in the unique repository of dishes and food

which has been mentioned heretofore in these
Sketches. Peering about the premises, Captain
Charley made a discovery. The modest little
parsonage stood on a steep incline, the upper side
resting on the red gravelly earth, while the lower
side was raised three or four feet from the ground.
The vacant space underneath had been used by
our several bachelor predecessors as a receptacle
for cast-off clothing. Malone, Lockley, and Evans, had thus disposed of their discarded apparel,
and Drury Bond and one or two other miners had
also added to the treasures that caught the eye of
the inquisitive Digger. It was a museum of sar-
torial curiosities — seedy and ripped broadcloth
coats, vests, and pants, flannel mining-shirts of gay
colors and of different degrees of wear and tear,
linen shirts that looked like battle-flags that had
been through the war, and old shoes and boots of
all sorts, from the high rubber water-proofs used by
miners to the ragged slippers that had adorned the
feet of the lonely single parsons whose names are
written above.

"Me take um?" asked Captain Charley, pointing to the treasure he had discovered.

Leave was given, and Captain Charley lost no
time in taking possession of the coveted goods.
He chuckled to himself as one article after another
was drawn forth from the pile which seemed to be

2

almost inexhaustible.   When he had gotten all out
and piled up together, it was a rare-looking sight.

"Mucho bueno!" exclaimed Captain Charley,
as he proceeded to array himself in a pair of trousers.   Then a shirt, then a vest, and then a coat,
were put on.   And then another, and another, and
yet another suit was donned in the same order.
He was fast becoming a "big Indian" indeed.   We
looked on and smiled, sympathizing with the evident delight of our visitor in his superabundant
wardrobe.   He was in full-dress, and enjoyed it.
But he made a failure at one point—his feet were
too large, or were not the right shape, for white
men's boots or shoes.   He tried several pairs, but
his huge flat foot would not enter them, and finally
he threw down the last one tried by him with a
Spanish exclamation not fit to be printed in these
pages.   That language is a musical one, but its
oaths are very harsh in sound.   A battered "stove-
pipe" hat was found among the spoils turned over
to Captain Charley.   Placing it on his head jaunt-
ily, he turned to us, saying, *Adios*, and went strut-
ting down the street, the picture of gratified vanity.   His appearance on Washington Street, the
main thoroughfare of the place, thus gorgeously
and abundantly arrayed, created a sensation.   It
was as good as a "show" to the jolly miners, always ready to be amused.   Captain Charley was

known to most of them, and they had a kindly feeling for the good-natured "fool Injun," as one of them called him in my hearing.

The next Digger I noticed was of the gentler (but in this case not lovelier) sex. She was an old squaw, who was in mourning. The sign of her grief was the black adobe mud spread over her face. She sat all day motionless and speechless, gazing up into the sky. Her grief was caused by the death of a child, and her sorrowful look showed that she had a mother's heart. Poor, degraded creature! What were her thoughts as she sat there looking so pitifully up into the silent, far-off heavens? All the livelong day she gazed thus fixedly into the sky, taking no notice of the passers-by, neither speaking, eating, nor drinking. It was a custom of the tribe, but its peculiar significance is unknown to me.

It was a great night at an adjoining camp when the old chief died. It was made the occasion of a fearful orgy. Dry wood and brush were gathered into a huge pile, the body of the dead chief was placed upon it, and the mass set on fire. As the flames blazed upward with a roar, the Indians, several hundred in number, broke forth into wild wailings and howlings, the shrill soprano of the women rising high above the din, as they marched around the burning pyre. Fresh fuel was supplied from time to time, and all night long the flames lighted up the surrounding hills which echoed with the shouts and howls of the savages. It was a touch of pandemonium. At dawn there was nothing left of the dead chief but ashes. The mourners took up their line of march toward the Stanislaus River, the squaws bearing their papooses on their backs, the "bucks" leading the way.

The Digger believes in a future life, and in future rewards and punishments. Good Indians and bad Indians are subjected to the same ordeal at death. Each one is rewarded according to his deeds.

The disembodied soul comes to a wide, turbid river, whose angry waters rush on to an unknown destination, roaring and foaming. From high banks on either side of the stream is stretched a pole smooth and small, over which he is required to walk. Upon the result of this *post-mortem* Blondinizing his fate depends. If he was in life a very good Indian he goes over safely, and finds on the other side a paradise, where the skies are cloudless, the air balmy, the flowers brilliant in color and sweet in perfume, the springs many and cool, and the deer plentiful and fat. In this fair clime there are no bad Indians, no briers, no snakes, no grizzly bears. Such is the paradise of good Diggers.

The Indian who was in life a mixed character, not all good or bad, but made up of both, starts across the fateful river, gets on very well until he reaches about half-way over, when his head becomes dizzy, and he tumbles into the boiling flood below. He swims for his life. (Every Indian on earth can swim, and he does not forget the art in the world of spirits.) Buffeting the waters, he is carried swiftly down the rushing current, and at last makes the shore, to find a country which, like his former life, is a mixture of good and bad. Some days are fair, and others are rainy and chilly; flowers and brambles grow together; there are some springs of water, but they are few, and not all cool and sweet; the deer are few, and shy, and lean, and grizzly bears roam the hills and valleys. This is the limbo of the moderately-wicked Digger.

The very bad Indian, placing his feet upon the attenuated bridge of doom, makes a few steps forward, stumbles, falls into the whirling waters below, and is swept downward with fearful velocity. At last, with desperate struggles he half swims, and is half washed ashore on the same side from which he started, to find a dreary land where the sun never shines, and the cold rains always pour down from the dark skies, where the water is brackish and foul, where no flowers ever bloom, where leagues may be traversed without seeing a deer, and grizzly bears abound. This is the hell of very bad Indians—and a very bad one it is.

The worst Indians of all, at death, are transformed into grizzly bears.

The Digger has a good appetite, and he is not particular about his eating. He likes grasshoppers, clover, acorns, roots, and fish. The flesh of a dead mule, horse, cow, or hog, does not come amiss to him—I mean the flesh of such as die natural deaths. He eats what he can get, and all he can get. In the grasshopper season he is fat and flourishing. In the suburbs of Sonora I came one day upon a lot of squaws, who were engaged in catching grasshoppers. Stretched along in line, armed with thick branches of pine, they threshed the ground in front of them as they advanced, driving the grasshoppers before them in constantly-increasing numbers, until the air was thick with the flying insects. Their course was directed to a deep gully, or gulch, into which they fell exhausted. It was astonishing to see with what dexterity the squaws would gather them up and thrust them into a sort of covered basket, made of willow-twigs or tule-grass, while the insects would be trying to escape, but would fall back unable to rise above the sides of the gulch in which they had been entrapped. The grasshoppers are dried, or cured, for winter use. A white man who had tried them told me they were pleasant eating, having a flavor very similar to that of a good shrimp. (I was content to take his word for it.)

When Bishop Soule was in California, in 1853, he paid a visit to a Digger campoody (or village) in the Calaveras hills. He was profoundly interested, and expressed an ardent desire to be instrumental in the conversion of one of these poor kin. It was yet early in the morning when the Bishop and his party arrived, and the Diggers were not astir, save here and there a squaw, in primitive array, who slouched lazily toward a spring of water hard by. But soon the arrival of the visitors was made known, and the bucks, squaws, and papooses, swarmed forth. They cast curious looks upon the whole party, but were specially struck with the majestic bearing of the Bishop, as were the passing crowds in London, who stopped in the streets to gaze with admiration upon the great American preacher. The Digger chief did not conceal his delight. After looking upon the Bishop fixedly for some moments, he went up to him, and tapping first his own chest and then the Bishop's, he said:

"Me big man—you big man!"

It was his opinion that two great men had met, and that the occasion was a grand one. Moralizers to the contrary notwithstanding, greatness is not always lacking in self-consciousness.

"I would like to go into one of their wigwams, or huts, and see how they really live," said the Bishop.

"You had better drop that idea," said the guide, a white man who knew more about Digger Indians than was good for his reputation and morals, but who was a good-hearted fellow, always ready to do a friendly turn, and with plenty of time on his hands to do it. The genius born to live without work will make his way by his wits, whether it be in the lobby at Washington City, or as a hanger-on at a Digger camp.

The Bishop insisted on going inside the chief's wigwam, which was a conical structure of long tule-grass, air-tight and weather-proof, with an aperture in front just large enough for a man's body in a crawling attitude. Sacrificing his dignity, the Bishop went down on all-fours, and then a degree lower, and, following the chief, crawled in. The air was foul, the smells were strong, and the light was dim. The chief proceeded to tender to his distinguished guest the hospitalities of the establishment, by offering to share his breakfast with him. The bill of fare was grasshoppers, with acorns as a side-dish. The Bishop maintained his dignity as he squatted there in the dirt—*his* dignity was equal to any test. He declined the grasshoppers tendered him by the chief, pleading that he had already breakfasted, but watched with peculiar sensations the movements of his host, as handful after handful of the crisp and juicy *gryllus vulgaris* were crammed into his capacious mouth, and swallowed. What he saw and smelt, and the absence of fresh air, began to tell upon the Bishop—he became sick and pale, while a gentle perspiration, like unto that felt in the beginning of seasickness, beaded his noble forehead. With slow dignity, but marked emphasis, he spoke:

"Brother Bristow, I propose that we retire."

They retired, and there is no record that Bishop Soule ever expressed the least desire to repeat his visit to the interior of a Digger Indian's abode.

The whites had many difficulties with the Diggers in the early days. In most cases I think the whites were chiefly to blame. It is very hard for the strong to be just to the weak. The weakest creature, pressed hard, will strike back. White women and children were massacred in retaliation for outrages committed upon the ignorant Indians by white outlaws. Then there would be a sweeping destruction of Indians by the excited whites, who in those days made rather light of Indian shooting. The shooting of a "buck" was about the same thing, whether it was a male Digger or a deer.

"There is not much fight in a Digger unless he's got the dead-wood on you, and then he'll make it rough for you. But these Injuns are of no use, and I'd about as soon shoot one of them as a coyote" (ki-o-te).

The speaker was a very red-faced, sandy-haired man, with blood-shot blue eyes, whom I met on his return to the Humboldt country after a visit to San Francisco.

"Did you ever shoot an Indian?" I asked.

"I first went up into the Eel River country in '46," he answered. "They give us a lot of trouble in them days. They would steal cattle, and our boys would shoot. But we've never had much difficulty with them since the big fight we had with them in 1849. A good deal of devilment had been goin' on all roun', and some had been killed on both sides. The Injuns killed two women on a ranch in the valley, and then we sot in just to wipe 'em out. Their camp was in a bend of the river, near the head of the valley, with a deep slough on the right flank. There was about sixty of us, and Dave —— was our captain. He was a hard rider, a dead shot, and not very tender-hearted. The boys sorter liked him, but kep' a sharp eye on him, knowin' he was so quick and handy with a pistol. Our plan was to git to their camp and fall on em at daybreak, but the sun was risin' just as we come in sight of it. A dog barked, and Dave sung out:

"'Out with your pistols! pitch in, and give 'em the hot lead!'

"In we galloped at full speed, and as the Injuns come out to see what was up, we let 'em have it. We shot forty bucks—about a dozen got away by swimmin' the river."

"Were any of the women killed?"

"A few were knocked over. You can't be particular when you are in a hurry; and a squaw, when her blood is up, will fight equal to a buck."

The fellow spoke with evident pride, feeling that he was detailing a heroic affair, having no idea that he had done any thing wrong in merely killing "bucks." I noticed that this same man was very kind to an old lady who took the stage for Bloomfield—helping her into the vehicle, and looking after her baggage. When we parted, I did not care to take the hand that had held a pistol that morning when the Digger camp was "wiped out."

The scattered remnants of the Digger tribes were gathered into a reservation in Round Valley, Mendocino county, north of the Bay of San Francisco, and were there taught a mild form of agricultural life, and put under the care of Government agents, contractors, and soldiers, with about

the usual results. One agent, who was also a
preacher, took several hundred of them into the
Christian Church. They seemed to have mastered
the leading facts of the gospel, and attained considerable proficiency in the singing of hymns. Altogether, the result of this effort at their conversion showed that they were human beings, and as
such could be made recipients of the truth and
grace of God, who is the Father of all the families of the earth. Their spiritual guide told me
he had to make one compromise with them—they
would dance. Extremes meet—the fashionable
white Christians of our gay capitals and the tawny
Digger exhibit the same weakness for the fascinat-
ing exercise that cost John the Baptist his head.

There is one thing a Digger cannot bear, and
that is the comforts and luxuries of civilized life.
A number of my friends, who had taken Digger
children to raise, found that as they approached
maturity they fell into a decline and died, in most
cases of some pulmonary affection. The only way
to save them was to let them rough it, avoiding
warm bed-rooms and too much clothing. A Digger girl belonged to my church at Santa Rosa,
and was a gentle, kind-hearted, grateful creature.
She was a domestic in the family of Colonel H——.
In that pleasant Christian household she developed
into a pretty fair specimen of brunette young

womanhood, but to the last she had an aversion to wearing shoes.

The Digger seems to be doomed. Civilization kills him; and if he sticks to his savagery, he will go down before the bullets, whisky, and vices of his white fellow-sinners.

THE CALIFORNIA MAD-HOUSE.

ON my first visit to the State Insane Asylum, at Stockton, I was struck by the beauty of a boy of some seven or eight years, who was moving about the grounds clad in a strait-jacket. In reply to my inquiries, the resident physician told me his history:

"About a year ago he was on his way to California with the family to which he belonged. He was a general pet among the passengers on the steamer. Handsome, confiding, and overflowing with boyish spirits, everybody had a smile and a kind word for the winning little fellow. Even the rough sailors would pause a moment to pat his curly head as they passed. One day a sailor, yielding to a playful impulse in passing, caught up the boy in his arms, crying;

"'I am going to throw you into the sea!'

"The child gave one scream of terror, and went into convulsions. When the paroxysm subsided,

(30)

he opened his eyes and gazed around with a vacant expression. His mother, who bent over him with a pale face, noticed the look, and almost screamed:

"'Tommy, here is your mother — do n't you know me?'

"The child gave no sign of recognition. He never knew his poor mother again. He was literally frightened out of his senses. The mother's anguish was terrible. The remorse of the sailor for his thoughtless freak was so great that it in some degree disarmed the indignation of the passengers and crew. The child had learned to read, and had made rapid progress in the studies suited to his age, but all was swept away by the cruel blow. He was unable to utter a word intelligently. Since he has been here, there have been signs of returning mental consciousness, and we have begun with him as with an infant. He knows and can call his own name, and is now learning the alphabet."

"How is his health?"

"His health is pretty good, except that he has occasional convulsive attacks that can only be controlled by the use of powerful opiates."

I was glad to learn, on a visit made two years later, that the unfortunate boy had died.

This child was murdered by a fool. The fools

are always murdering children, though the work is not always done as effectually as in this case. They cripple and half kill them by terror. There are many who will read this Sketch who will carry to the grave, and into the world of spirits, natures out of which half the sweetness, and brightness, and beauty has been crushed by ignorance or brutality. In most cases it is ignorance. The hand that should guide, smites; the voice that should soothe, jars the sensitive chords that are untuned forever. He who thoughtlessly excites terror in a child's heart is unconsciously doing the devil's work; he that does it consciously is a devil.

"There is a lady here whom I wish you would talk to. She belongs to one of the most respectable families in San Francisco, is cultivated, refined, and has been the center of a large and loving circle. Her monomania is spiritual despair. She thinks she has committed the unpardonable sin. There she is now. I will introduce you to her. Talk with her, and comfort her if you can."

She was a tall, well-formed woman in black, with all the marks of refinement in her dress and bearing. She was walking the floor to and fro with rapid steps, wringing her hands, and moaning piteously. Indescribable anguish was in her face—it was a *hopeless* face. It haunted my thoughts for many days, and it is vividly before me as I write now. The kind physician introduced me, and left the apartment.

There is a sacredness about such an interview that inclines me to veil its details.

"I am willing to talk with you, sir, and appreciate your motive, but I understand my situation. I have committed the unpardonable sin, and I know there is no hope for me."

With the earnestness excited by intense sympathy, I combated her conclusion, and felt certain that I could make her see and feel that she had given way to an illusion. She listened respectfully to all I had to say, and then said again:

"I know my situation. I denied my Saviour after all his goodness to me, and he has left me forever."

There was the frozen calmness of utter despair in look and tone. I left her as I found her.

"I will introduce you to another woman, the opposite of the poor lady you have just seen. She thinks she is a queen, and is perfectly harmless. You must be careful to humor her illusion. There she is—let me present you."

She was a woman of immense size, enormously fat, with broad red face, and a self-satisfied smirk, dressed in some sort of flaming scarlet stuff, profusely tinseled all over, making a gorgeously ridic-

3

ulous effect. She received me with a mixture of mock dignity and smiling condescension, and surveying herself admiringly, she asked:

"How do you like my dress?"

It was not the first time that royalty had shown itself not above the little weaknesses of human nature. On being told that her apparel was indeed magnificent, she was much pleased, and drew herself up proudly, and was a picture of ecstatic vanity. Are the real queens as happy? When they lay aside their royal robes for their grave-clothes, will not the pageantry which was the glory of their lives seem as vain as that of this tinseled queen of the mad-house? Where is happiness, after all? Is it in the circumstances, the external conditions? or, is it in the mind? Such were the thoughts passing through my mind, when a man approached with a violin. Every eye brightened, and the queen seemed to thrill with pleasure in every nerve.

"This is the only way we can get some of them to take any exercise. The music rouses them, and they will dance as long as they are permitted to do so."

The fiddler struck up a lively tune, and the queen, with marvelous lightness of step and ogling glances, ambled up to a tall, raw-boned Methodist preacher, who had come with me, and invited him to dance with her. The poor parson seemed sadly embarrassed, as her manner was very pressing, but he awkwardly and confusedly declined, amid the titters of all present. It was a singular spectacle, that dance of the mad-women. The most striking figure on the floor was the queen. Her great size, her brilliant apparel, her astonishing agility, the perfect time she kept, the bows, the smiles and blandishments, she bestowed on an imaginary partner, were indescribably ludicrous. Now and then, in her evolutions, she would cast a momentary reproachful glance at the ungallant clergyman who had refused to dance with feminine royalty, and who stood looking on with a sheepish expression of face. He was a Kentuckian, and lack of gallantry is not a Kentucky trait.

During the session of the Annual Conference at Stockton, in 1859 or 1860, the resident physician invited me to preach to the inmates of the Asylum on Sunday afternoon. The novelty of the service, which was announced in the daily papers, attracted a large number of visitors, among them the greater part of the preachers. The day was one of those bright, clear, beautiful October days, peculiar to California, that make you think of heaven. I stood on the steps, and the hundreds of men and women stood below me, with their upturned faces. Among them were old men crushed by sorrow, and old men ruined by vice; aged women with faces that seemed to plead for pity, women that made you shrink from their unwomanly gaze; lion-like young men, made for heroes but caught in the devil's trap and changed into beasts; and boys whose looks showed that sin had already stamped them with its foul insignia, and burned into their souls the shame which is to be one of the elements of its eternal punishment. A less impressible man than I would have felt moved at the sight of that throng of bruised and broken creatures. A hymn was read, and when Burnet, Kelsay, Neal, and others of the preachers, struck up an old tune, voice after voice joined in the melody until it swelled into a mighty volume of sacred song. I noticed that the faces of many were wet with tears, and there was an indescribable pathos in their voices. The pitying God, amid the rapturous halleluiahs of the heavenly hosts, bent to listen to the music of these broken harps. This text was announced, *My peace I give unto you;* and the sermon began.

Among those standing nearest to me was "Old Kelley," a noted patient, whose monomania was the notion that he was a millionaire, and who spent most of his time in drawing checks on imaginary deposits for vast sums of money. I held one of his checks for a round million, but it has never yet been cashed. The old man pressed up close to me, seeming to feel that the success of the service somehow depended on him. I had not more than fairly begun my discourse, when he broke in:

"That's Daniel Webster!"

I don't mind a judicious "Amen," but this put me out a little. I resumed my remarks, and was getting another good start, when he again broke in enthusiastically:

"Henry Clay!"

The preachers standing around me smiled—I think I heard one or two of them titter. I could not take my eyes from Kelley, who stood with open mouth and beaming countenance, waiting for me to go on. He held me with an evil fascination. I did go on in a louder voice, and in a sort of desperation; but again my delighted hearer exclaimed:

"Calhoun!"

"Old Kelley" spoiled that sermon, though he meant kindly. He died not long afterward, gloating over his fancied millions to the last.

"If you have steady nerves, come with me and I will show you the worst case we have—a woman half tigress, and half devil."

Ascending a stair-way, I was led to an angle of the building assigned to the patients whose violence required them to be kept in close confinement.

"Hark! do n't you hear her? She is in one of her paroxysms now."

The sounds that issued from one of the cells were like nothing I had ever heard before. They were a series of unearthly, fiendish shrieks, intermingled with furious imprecations, as of a lost spirit in an ecstasy of rage and fear.

The face that glared upon me through the iron grating was hideous, horrible. It was that of a woman, or of what had been a woman, but was now a wreck out of which evil passion had stamped all that was womanly or human. I involuntarily shrunk back as I met the glare of those fiery eyes, and caught the sound of words that made me shudder. I never suspected myself of being a coward, but I felt glad that the iron bars of the cell against which she dashed herself were strong. I had read of Furies—one was now before me. The bloated, gin-inflamed face, the fiery-red, wicked eyes, the swinish chin, the tangled coarse hair falling around her like writhing snakes, the tiger-like clutch of her dirty fingers, the horrible words—the picture was sickening, disgust for the time almost extinguishing pity.

"She was the keeper of a beer-saloon in San Francisco, and led a life of drunkenness and licentiousness until she broke down, and she was brought here."

"Is there any hope of her restoration?"

"I fear not — nothing short of a miracle can re-tune an instrument so fearfully broken and jangled."

I thought of her out of whom were cast the seven devils, and of Him who came to seek and to save the lost, and resisting the impulse that prompted me to hurry away from the sight and hearing of this lost woman, I tried to talk with her, but had to retire at last amid a volley of such language as I hope never to hear from a woman's lips again.

"Listen! Did you ever hear a sweeter voice than that?"

I had heard the voice before, and thrilled under its power. It was a female voice of wonderful richness and volume, with a touch of something in it that moved you strangely—a sort of intensity that set your pulses to beating faster, while it entranced you. The whole of the spacious grounds were flooded with the melody, and the passing teamsters on the public highway would pause and listen with wonder and delight. The singer was a fair young girl, with dark auburn hair, large brown eyes, that were at times dreamy and sad, and then again lit up with excitement, as her moods changed from sad to gay.

"She will sit silent for hours gazing listlessly out of the window, and then all at once break forth into a burst of song so sweet and thrilling that the other patients gather near her and listen in rapt silence and delight. Sometimes at a dead hour of the night her voice is heard, and then it seems that she is under a special *afflatus*—she seems to be inspired by the very soul of music, and her songs, wild and sad, wailing and rollicking, by turns, but all exquisitely sweet, fill the long night-hours with their melody."

The shock caused by the sudden death of her betrothed lover overthrew her reason, and blighted her life. By the mercy of God, the love of music and the gift of song survived the wreck of love and of reason. This girl's voice, pealing forth upon the still summer evening air, is mingled with my last recollection of Stockton and its refuge for the doubly miserable who are doomed to death in life.

SAN QUENTIN.

"I WANT you to go with me over to San Quentin next Thursday, and preach a thanksgiving-sermon to the poor fellows in the State-prison."

On the appointed morning, I met our party at the Vallejo-street wharf, and we were soon steaming on our way. Passing under the guns of Fort Alcatraz, past Angel Island—why so called I know not, as in early days it was inhabited not by angels but goats only—all of us felt the exhilaration of the California sunshine, and the bracing November air, as we stood upon the guards, watching the play of the lazy-looking porpoises, that seemed to roll along, keeping up with the swift motion of the boat in such a leisurely way. The porpoise is a deceiver. As he rolls up to the surface of the water, in his lumbering way, he looks as if he were a huge lump of unwieldy awkwardness, floating at random and almost helpless; but when you come to know him better, you find that he is

(41)

a marvel of muscular power and swiftness. I have seen a "school" of porpoises in the Pacific swimming for hours alongside one of our fleetest ocean-steamers, darting a few yards ahead now and then, as if by mere volition, cutting their way through the water with the directness of an arrow. The porpoise is playful at times, and his favorite game is a sort of leap-frog. A score or more of the creatures, seemingly full of fun and excitement, will chase one another at full speed, throwing themselves from the water and turning somersaults in the air, the water boiling with the agitation, and their huge bodies flashing in the light. You might almost imagine that they had found something in the sea that had made them drunk, or that they had inhaled some sort of piscatorial anæsthetic. But here we are at our destination. The bell rings, we round to, and land.

At San Quentin nature is at her best, and man at his worst. Against the rocky shore the waters of the bay break in gentle plashings when the winds are quiet. When the gales from the southwest sweep through the Golden Gate, and set the white caps to dancing to their wild music, the waves rise high, and dash upon the dripping stones with a hoarse roar, as of anger. Beginning a few hundreds of yards from the water's edge, the hills slope up, and up, and up, until they touch the base of Tamelpais, on whose dark and rugged summit, four thousand feet above the sea that laves his feet on the west, the rays of the morning sun fall with transfiguring glory while yet the valley below lies in shadow. On this lofty pinnacle linger the last rays of the setting sun, as it drops into the bosom of the Pacific. In stormy weather, the mist and clouds roll in from the ocean, and gather in dark masses around his awful head, as if the sea-gods had risen from their homes in the deep, and were holding a council of war amid the battle of the elements; at other times, after calm, bright days, the thin, soft white clouds that hang about his crest deepen into crimson and gold, and the mountain-top looks as if the angels of God had come down to encamp, and pitched here their pavilions of glory. This is nature at San Quentin, and this is Tamelpais as I have looked upon it many a morning and many an evening from my window above the sea at North Beach.

The gate is opened for us, and we enter the prison-walls. It is a holiday, and the day is fair and balmy; but the chill and sadness cannot be shaken off, as we look around us. The sunshine seems almost to be a mockery in this place where fellow-men are caged and guarded like wild beasts, and skulk about with shaved heads, clad in the striped uniform of infamy. Merciful God! is this what thy creature man was made for? How long, how long?

Seated upon the platform with the prison officials and visitors, I watched my strange auditors as they came in. There were one thousand of them. Their faces were a curious study. Most of them were bad faces. Beast and devil were printed on them. Thick necks, heavy back-heads, and low, square foreheads, were the prevalent types. The least repulsive were those who looked as if they were all animal, creatures of instinct and appetite, good-natured and stupid; the most repulsive were those whose eyes had a gleam of mingled sensuality and ferocity. But some of these faces that met my gaze were startling—they seemed so out of place. One old man with gray hair, pale, sad face, and clear blue eyes, might have passed, in other garb and in other company, for an honored member of the Society of Friends. He had killed a man in a mountain county. If he was indeed a murderer at heart, nature had given him the wrong imprint. My attention was struck by a smooth-faced, handsome young fellow, scarcely of age, who looked as little like a convict as anybody on that platform. He was in for burglary, and had a very bad record. Some came in half laughing, as if they thought the whole affair more a joke than any thing else. The Mexicans, of whom there was quite a number, were sullen and scowling. There is gloom in the Spanish blood. The irrepressible good nature of several ruddy-faced Irishmen broke out in sly merriment. As the service began, the discipline of the prison showed itself in the quiet that instantly prevailed; but only a few, who joined in the singing, seemed to feel the slightest interest in it. Their eyes were wandering, and their faces were vacant. They had the look of men who had come to be talked at and patronized, and who were used to it. The prayer that was offered was not calculated to banish such a feeling—it was dry and cold. I stood up to begin the sermon. Never before had I realized so fully that God's message was to lost men, and for lost men. A mighty tide of pity rushed in upon my soul as I looked down into the faces of my hearers. My eyes filled, and my heart melted within me. I could not speak until after a pause, and only then by great effort. There was a deep silence, and every face was lifted to mine as I announced the text. God had touched my heart and theirs at the start. I read the words slowly: *God hath not appointed us to wrath, but to obtain salvation by our Lord Jesus Christ.* Then I said:

"My fellow-men, I come to you to-day with a message from my Father, and your Father in heaven. It is a message of hope. God help me to deliver it as I ought! God help you to hear it as you ought! I will not insult you by saying that because you have an extra dinner, a few hours respite from your toil, and a little fresh air and sunshine, you ought to have a joyful thanksgiving to-day. If I should talk thus, you would be ready to ask me how I would like to change places with you. You would despise me, and I would despise myself, for indulging in such cant. Your lot is a hard one. The battle of life has gone against you—whether by your own fault or by hard fortune, it matters not, so far as the fact is concerned; this thanksgiving-day finds you locked in here, with broken lives, and wearing the badge of crime. God alone knows the secrets of each throbbing heart before me, and how it is that you have come to this. Fellow-men, children of my Father in heaven, putting myself for the moment in your place, the bitterness of your lot is real and terrible to me. For some of you there is no happier prospect for this life than to toil within these walls by day, and sleep in yonder cells by night, through the weary, slow-dragging years, and then to die, with only the hands of hired attendants to wipe the death-sweat from your brows; and then to be put in a convict's coffin, and taken up on the hill yonder, and laid in a lonely grave. My God! this is terrible!"

An unexpected dramatic effect followed these words. The heads of many of the convicts fell forward on their breasts, as if struck with sudden paralysis. They were the men who were in for life, and the horror of it overcame them. The silence was broken by sobbings all over the room. The officers and visitors on the platform were weeping. The angel of pity hovered over the place, and the glow of human sympathy had melted those stony hearts. A thousand strong men were thrilled with the touch of sympathy, and once more the sacred fountain of tears was unsealed. These convicts were men, after all, and deep down under the rubbish of their natures there was still burning the spark of a humanity not yet extinct. It was wonderful to see the softened expression of their faces. Yes, they were men, after all, responding to the voice of sympathy, which had been but too strange to many of them all their evil lives. Many of them had inherited hard conditions; they were literally conceived in sin and born in iniquity; they grew up in the midst of vice. For them pure and holy lives were a moral impossibility. Evil with them was hereditary, organic, and the result of association; it poisoned their blood at the start, and stamped itself on their features from their cradles. Human law, in dealing with these victims of evil circumstance, can make little discrimination. Society must protect itself, treating a criminal as a criminal. But what will God do with them hereafter? Be sure he will do right. Where little is given, little will be required. It shall be better for Tyre and Sidon at the day of judgment than for Chorazin and Bethsaida. There is no ruin without remedy, except that which a man makes for himself by abusing mercy, and throwing away proffered opportunity. Thoughts like these rushed through the preacher's mind, as he stood there looking in the tear-bedewed faces of these men of crime. A fresh tide of pity rose in his heart, that he felt came from the heart of the all-pitying One.

"I do not try to disguise from you, or from myself the fact that for this life your outlook is not bright. But I come to you this day with a message of hope from God our Father. He hath not appointed you to wrath. He loves all his children. He sent his Son to die for them. Jesus trod the paths of pain, and drained the cup of sorrow. He died as a malefactor, for malefactors. He died for me. He died for each one of you. If I knew the most broken, the most desolate-hearted, despairing man before me, who feels that he is scorned of men and forsaken of God, I would go to where he sits and put my hand on his head, and tell him that God hath not appointed him to wrath, but to obtain salvation by our Lord Jesus Christ, who died for us. I would tell him that his Father in heaven loves him still, loves him more than the mother that bore him. I would tell him that all the wrongs and follies of his past life may from this hour be turned into so much capital of a warning experience, and that a million of years from to-day he may be a child of the Heavenly Father, and an heir of glory, having the freedom of the heavens and the blessedness of everlasting life. O brothers, God does love you! Nothing can ruin you but your own despair. No man has any right to despair who has eternity before him. Eternity? Long, long eternity! Blessed, blessed eternity! That is yours—all of it. It may be a happy eternity for each one of you. From this moment you may begin a better life. There is hope for you, and mercy, and love, and heaven. This is the message I bring you warm from a brother's heart, and warm from the heart of Jesus, whose life-blood was poured out for you and me. His loving hand opened the gate of mercy and hope to every man. The proof is that he died for us. O Son of God, take us to thy pitying arms, and lift us up into the light that never, never grows dim—into the love that fills heaven and eternity!"

As the speaker sunk into his seat, there was a silence that was almost painful for a few moments.

4

Then the pent-up emotion of the men broke forth in sobs that shook their strong frames. Dr. Lucky, the prisoner's friend, made a brief, tearful prayer, and then the benediction was said, and the service was at an end. The men sat still in their seats. As we filed out of the chapel, many hands were extended to grasp mine, holding it with a clinging pressure. I passed out bearing with me the impression of an hour I can never forget; and the images of those thousand faces are still painted in memory.

"CORRALED."

"SO you were *corraled* last night?"

This was the remark of a friend whom I met in the streets of Stockton the morning after my adventure. I knew what the expression meant as applied to cattle, but I, had never heard it before in reference to a human being. Yes, I had been *corraled;* and this is how it happened:

It was in the old days, before there were any railroads in California. With a wiry, clean-limbed pinto horse, I undertook to drive from Sacramento City to Stockton one day. It was in the winter season, and the clouds were sweeping up from the south-west, the snow-crested Sierras hidden from sight by dense masses of vapor boiling at their bases and massed against their sides. The roads were heavy from the effects of previous rains, and the plucky little pinto sweated as he pulled through the long stretches of black adobe mud. A cold wind struck me in the face, and the ride was a

(51)

dreary one from the start.   But I pushed on confidently, having faith in the spotted mustang, despite the evident fact that he had lost no little of the spirit with which he dashed out of town at starting.   When a genuine mustang flags, it is a serious business.   The hardiness and endurance of this breed of horses almost exceed belief.

Toward night a cold rain began to fall, driving in my face with the head-wind.   Still many a long mile lay between me and Stockton.   Dark came on, and it was dark indeed.   The outline of the horse I was driving could not be seen, and the flat country through which I was driving was a great black sea of night.   I trusted to the instinct of the horse, and moved on.   The bells of a wagon-team meeting me fell upon my ear.   I called out,

"Halloo there!"

"What's the matter?" answered a heavy voice through the darkness.

"Am I in the road to Stockton, and can I get there to-night?"

"You are in the road, but you will never find your way such a night as this.   It is ten good miles from here; you have several bridges to cross —you had better stop at the first house you come to, about half a mile ahead.   I am going to strike camp myself."

I thanked my adviser, and went on, hearing the

sound of the tinkling bells, but unable to see any thing. In a little while I saw a light ahead, and was glad to see it. Driving up in front and halting, I repeated the traveler's "halloo" several times, and at last got a response in a hoarse, gruff voice.

"I am belated on my way to Stockton, and am cold, and tired, and hungry. Can I get shelter with you for the night?"

"You may try it, if you want to," answered the unmusical voice abruptly.

In a few moments a man appeared to take the horse, and taking my satchel in hand, I went into the house. The first thing that struck my attention on entering the room was a big log-fire, which I was glad to see, for I was wet and very cold. Taking a chair in the corner, I looked around. The scene that presented itself was not reässuring. The main feature of the room was a bar, with an ample supply of barrels, demijohns, bottles, tumblers, and all the *et cæteras*. Behind the counter stood the proprietor, a burly fellow with a buffalo-neck, fair skin and blue eyes, with a frightful scar across his left under-jaw and neck; his shirt-collar was open, exposing a huge chest, and his sleeves were rolled up above the elbows. I noticed also that one of his hands was minus all the fingers but the half of one—the result probably of some

desperate rencounter. I did not like the appearance of my landlord, and he eyed me in a way
that led me to fear that he liked my looks as little as
I did his; but the claims of other guests soon divert-
ed his attention from me, and I was left to get
warm and make further observations. At a table
in the middle of the room several hard-looking
fellows were betting at cards, amid terrible profanity and frequent drinks of whisky. They cast
inquiring and not very friendly glances at me from
time to time, once or twice exchanging whispers
and giggling. As their play went on, and tumbler
after tumbler of whisky was drunk by them, they
became more boisterous. Threats were made of
using pistols and knives, with which they all
seemed to be heavily armed; and one sottish-look-
ing brute actually drew forth a pistol, but was
disarmed in no gentle way by the big-limbed landlord. The profanity and other foul language were
horrible. Many of my readers have no conception
of the brutishness of men when whisky and Satan
have full possession of them. In the midst of a
volley of oaths and terrible imprecations by one
of the most violent of the set, there was a faint
gleam of lingering decency exhibited by one of
his companions:

"Blast it, Dick, *do n't cuss so loud*—that fellow
in the corner there is a preacher!"

There was some potency in "the cloth" even there. How he knew my calling I do not know. The remark directed particular attention to me, and I became unpleasantly conspicuous. Scowling glances were bent upon me by two or three of the ruffians, and one fellow made a profane remark not at all complimentary to my vocation—whereat there was some coarse laughter. In the meantime I was conscious of being very hungry. My hunger, like that of a boy, is a very positive thing—at least it was very much so in those days. Glancing toward the maimed and scarred giant who stood behind the bar, I found he was gazing at me with a fixed expression.

"Can I get something to eat? I am very hungry, sir," I said in my blandest tones.

"Yes, we've plenty of cold goose, and may be Pete can pick up something else for you if he is sober and in a good humor. Come this way."

I followed him through a narrow passage-way, which led to a long, low-ceiled room, along nearly the whole length of which was stretched a table, around which were placed rough stools for the rough men about the place.

Pete, the cook, came in, and the head of the house turned me over to him, and returned to his duties behind the bar. From the noise of the uproar going on, his presence was doubtless needed.

Pete set before me a large roasted wild-goose, not badly cooked, with bread, milk, and the inevitable cucumber pickles. The knives and forks were not very bright—in fact, they had been subjected to influences promotive of oxidation; and the dishes were not free from signs of former use. Nothing could be said against the table-cloth—there was no table-cloth there. But the goose was fat, brown, and tender; and a hungry man defers his criticisms until he is done eating. That is what I did. Pete evidently regarded me with curiosity. He was about fifty years of age, and had the look of a man who had come down in the world. His face bore the marks of the effects of strong drink, but it was not a bad face; it was more weak than wicked.

"Are you a preacher?" he asked.

".I thought so," he added, after getting my answer to his question. "Of what persuasion are you?" he further inquired.

When I told him I was a Methodist, he said quickly and with some warmth:

"I was sure of it. This is a rough place for a man of your calling. Would you like some eggs? we've plenty on hand. And may be you would like a cup of coffee," he added, with increasing hospitality.

I took the eggs, but declined the coffee, not liking the looks of the cups and saucers, and not caring to wait.

"I used to be a Methodist myself," said Pete, with a sort of choking in his throat, "but bad luck and bad company have brought me down to this. I have a family in Iowa, a wife and four children. I guess they think I'm dead, and sometimes I wish I was."

Pete stood by my chair, actually crying. The sight of a Methodist preacher brought up old times. He told me his story. He had come to California hoping to make a fortune in a hurry, but had only ill luck from the start. His prospectings were always failures, his partners cheated him, his health broke down, his courage gave way, and—he faltered a little, and then spoke it out— he took to whisky, and then the worst came.

"I have come down to this—cooking for a lot of roughs at five dollars a week, and all the whisky I want. It would have been better for me if I had died when I was in the hospital at San Andreas."

Poor Pete! he had indeed touched bottom. But he had a heart and a conscience still, and my own heart warmed toward my poor backslidden brother.

"You are not a lost man yet. You are worth a thousand dead men. You can get out of this, and you must. You must act the part of a brave man, and not be any longer a coward. Bad luck and lack of success are a disgrace to no man. There is where you went wrong. It was cowardly to give up and not write to your family, and then take to whisky."

"I know all that, Elder. There is no better little woman on earth than my wife"—Pete choked up again.

"You write to her this very night, and go back to her and your children just as soon as you can get the money to pay your way. Act the man, and all will come right yet. I have writing-materials here in my satchel—pen, ink, paper, envelopes, stamps, every thing; I am an editor, and go fixed up for writing."

The letter was written, I acting as Pete's amanuensis, he pleading that he was a poor scribe at best, and that his nerves were too unsteady for such work. Taking my advice, he made a clean breast of the whole matter, throwing himself on the forgiveness of the wife whom he had so shamefully neglected, and promising by the help of God to make all the amends possible in time to come. The letter was duly directed, sealed, and stamped, and Pete looked as if a great weight had been lifted from his soul. He had made me a fire in the little stove, saying it was better than the bar-room; in which opinion I was fully agreed.

"There is no place for you to sleep to-night without *corraling* you with the fellows; there is but one bed-room, and there are fourteen bunks in it."

I shuddered at the prospect—fourteen bunks in one small room, and those whisky-sodden, loud-cursing card-players to be my room-mates for the night!

"I prefer sitting here by the stove all night," I said; "I can employ most of the time writing, if I can have a light."

Pete thought a moment, looked grave, and then said:

"That won't do, Elder; those fellows would take offense, and make trouble. Several of them are out now goose-hunting; they will be coming in at all hours from now till day-break, and it won't do for them to find you sitting up here alone. The best thing for you to do is to go in and take one of those bunks; you need n't take off any thing but your coat and boots, and"—here he lowered his voice, looking about him as he spoke—"*if you have any money about, keep it next to your body.*"

The last words were spoken with peculiar emphasis.

Taking the advice given me, I took up my baggage and followed Pete to the room where I was to spend the night. Ugh! it was dreadful. The single window in the room was nailed down, and the air was close and foul. The bunks were damp and dirty beyond belief, grimed with foulness, and recking with ill odors. This was being *corraled*. I turned to Pete, saying:

"I can't stand this—I will go back to the kitchen."

"You had better follow my advice, Elder," said he very gravely. "I know things about here better than you do. It's rough, but you had better stand it."

And I did; being *corraled*, I had to stand it. That fearful night! The drunken fellows staggered in one by one, cursing and hiccoughing, until every bunk was occupied. They muttered oaths in their sleep, and their stertorous breathings made a concert fit for Tartarus. The sickening odors of whisky, onions, and tobacco filled the room. I lay there and longed for daylight, which seemed as if it never would come. I thought of the descriptions I· had heard and read of hell, and just then the most vivid conception of its horror was to be shut up forever with the aggregated impurity of the universe. By contrast I tried to think of that city of God into which, it is said, "there shall in no wise enter into it any thing that defileth, neither whatsoever worketh abomination, or maketh a lie; but they which are written in the Lamb's book of life." But thoughts of heaven did not suit· the situation; it was more suggestive of the other place. The horror of being shut up eternally in hell as the companion of lost spirits was intensified by the experience and reflections of that night when I was *corraled.*

Day came at last. I rose with the first streaks of the dawn, and not having much toilet to make, I was soon out-of-doors. Never did I breathe the pure, fresh air with such profound pleasure and gratitude. I drew deep inspirations, and, opening my coat and vest, let the breeze that swept up the valley blow upon me unrestricted. How bright, was the face of nature, and how sweet her breath after the sights, sounds, and smells of the night!

I did not wait for breakfast, but had my pinto and buggy brought out, and, bidding Pete good-by, hurried on to Stockton.

"So you were *corraled* last night?" was the remark of a friend, quoted at the beginning of this true sketch. "What was the name of the proprietor of the house?"

I gave him the name.

"Dave W——!" he exclaimed with fresh astonishment. "That is the roughest place in the San Joaquin Valley. Several men have been killed and robbed there during the last two or three years."

I hope Pete got back safe to his wife and children in Iowa; and I hope I may never be *corraled* again.

THE REBLOOMING.

IT is now more than twenty years since the morning a slender youth of handsome face and modest mien came into my office on the corner of Montgomery and Clay streets, San Francisco. He was the son of a preacher well known in Missouri and California, a man of rare good sense, caustic wit, and many eccentricities. The young man became an *attaché* of my newspaper-office and an inmate of my home. He was as fair as a girl, and refined in his taste and manners. A genial taciturnity, if the expression may be allowed, marked his bearing in the social circle. Everybody had a kind feeling and a good word for the quiet, bright-faced youth. In the discharge of his duties in the office he was punctual and trustworthy, showing not only industry but unusual aptitude for business. It was with special pleasure that I learned that he was turning his thoughts to the subject of religion. During the services in the little Pine-street church

(62)

he would sit with thoughtful face, and not seldom
with moistened eyes. He read the Bible and
prayed in secret. I was not surprised when he
came to me one day and opened his heart. The
great crisis in his life had come. God was speaking to his soul, and he was listening to his voice.
The uplifted cross drew him, and he yielded to the
gentle attraction. We prayed together, and henceforth there was a new and sacred bond that bound
us to each other. I felt that I was a witness to
the most solemn transaction that can take place
on earth — the wedding of a soul to a heavenly
faith. Soon thereafter he went to Virginia, to attend college. There he united with the Church.
His letters to me were full of gratitude and joy.
It was the blossoming of his spiritual life, and the
air was full of its fragrance, and the earth was
flooded with glory. A pedestrian-tour among the
Virginia hills brought him into communion with
Nature at a time when it was rapture to drink in
its beauty and its grandeur. The light kindled
within his soul by the touch of the Holy Spirit
transfigured the scenery upon which he gazed, and
the glory of God shone round about the young
student in the flush and blessedness of his first
love. O blessed days! O days of brightness, and
sweetness, and rapture! The soul is then in its
blossoming-time, and all high enthusiasms, all

bright dreams, all thrilling joys, are realities which
inwork themselves into the consciousness, to be forgotten never; to remain with us as prophecies of
the eternal spring-time that awaits the true-hearted
on the hills of God beyond the grave, or as accus-
ing voices charging us with the murder of our
dead ideals! Amid the dust and din of the battle
in after-years we turn to this radiant spot in our
journey with smiles or tears, according as we have
been true or false to the impulses, aspirations, and
purposes inspired within us by that first, and
brightest, and nearest manifestation of God. Such
a season is as natural to every life as the April
buds and June roses are to forest and garden. The
spring-time of some lives is deferred by unpropi-
tious circumstance to the time when it should be
glowing with autumnal glory, and rich in the fruit-
age of the closing year. The life that does not
blossom into religion in youth may have light at
noon, and peace at sunset, but misses the morning
glory on the hills, and the dew that sparkles on
grass and flower. The call of God to the young
to seek him early is the expression of a true psy-
chology no less than of a love infinite in its depth
and tenderness.

His college-course finished, my young friend returned to California, and in one of its beautiful
valley-towns he entered a law-office, with a view

to prepare himself for the legal profession. Here he was thrown into daily association with a little knot of skeptical lawyers. As is often the case, their moral obliquities ran parallel with their errors in opinion. They swore, gambled genteelly, and drank. It is not strange that in this icy atmosphere the growth of my young friend in the Christian life was stunted. Such influences are like the dreaded north wind that at times sweeps over the valleys of California in the spring and early summer, blighting and withering the vegetation it does not kill. The brightness of his hope was dimmed, and his soul knew the torture of doubt—a torture that is always keenest to him who allows himself to sink in the region of fogs after he has once stood upon the sunlit summit of faith. Just at this crisis, a thing little in itself deepened the shadow that was falling upon his life. A personal misunderstanding with the pastor kept him from attending church. Thus he lost the most effectual defense against the assaults that were being made upon his faith and hope, in being separated from the fellowship and cut off from the activities of the Church of God. Have you not noted these malign coincidences in life? There are times when it seems that the tide of events sets against us—when, like the princely sufferer of the land of Uz, every messenger that crosses the

5

threshold brings fresh tidings of ill, and our whole destiny seems to be rushing to a predoomed perdition. The worldly call it bad luck; the superstitious call it fate; the believer in God calls it by another name. Always of a delicate constitution, my friend now exhibited symptoms of serious pulmonary disease. It was at that time the fashion in California to prescribe whisky as a specific for that class of ailments. It is possible that there is virtue in the prescription, but I am sure of one thing, namely, that if consumption diminished, drunkenness increased; if fewer died of phthisis, more died of *delirium tremens.* The physicians of California have sent a host of victims raving and gibbering in drunken frenzy or idiocy down to death and hell! I have reason to believe that my friend inherited a constitutional weakness at this point. As flame to tinder, was the medicinal whisky to him. It grew upon him rapidly, and soon this cloud overshadowed all his life. He struggled hard to break the serpent-folds that were tightening around him; but the fire that had been kindled seemed to be quenchless. An uncontrolled evil passion is hell-fire. He writhed in its burnings in an agony that could be understood only by such as knew how almost morbidly sensitive was his nature, and how vital was his conscience. I became a pastor in the town where he lived, and renewed my association with him as far as I could. But there was a constraint unlike the old times. When under the influence of liquor, he would pass me in the streets with his head down, a deeper flush mantling his cheek as he hurried by with unsteady step. Sometimes I met him staggering homeward through a back street, hiding from the gaze of men. He was at first shy of me when sober, but gradually the constraint wore off, and he seemed disposed to draw nearer to me, as in the old days. His struggle went on, days of drunkenness following weeks of soberness, his haggard face after each debauch wearing a look of unspeakable weariness and wretchedness. One of the lawyers who had led him into the mazes of doubt—a man of large and versatile gifts, whose lips were touched with a noble and persuasive eloquence—sunk deeper and deeper into the black depths of drunkenness, until the tragedy ended in a horror that lessened the gains of the saloons for at least a few days. He was found dead in his bed one morning in a pool of blood, his throat cut by his own guilty hand.

My friend had married a lovely girl, and the cottage in which they lived was one of the cosiest, and the garden in front was a little paradise of neatness and beauty. Ah! I must drop a veil over a part of this true tale. All along I have written under half protest, the image of a sad, wistful face rising at times between my eyes and the sheet on which these words are traced. They loved each other tenderly and deeply, and both were conscious of the presence of the devil that was turning their heaven into hell.

"Save him, Doctor, save him! He is the noblest of men, and the tenderest, truest husband. He loves you, and he will let you talk to him. Save him, O save him! Help me to pray for him! My heart will break!"

Poor child! her loving heart was indeed breaking; and her fresh young life was crushed under a weight of grief and shame too heavy to be borne.

What *he* said to me in the interviews held in his sober intervals I have not the heart to repeat now. He still fought against his enemy; he still buffeted the billows that were going over him, though with feebler stroke. When their little child died, her tears fell freely, but he was like one stunned. Stony and silent he stood and saw the little grave filled up, and rode away tearless, the picture of hopelessness.

By a coincidence, after my return to San Francisco, he came thither, and again became my neighbor at North Beach. I went up to see him one evening. He was very feeble, and it was plain that the end was not far off. At the first glance I saw that a great change had taken place in him.

He had found his lost self. The strong drink was shut out from him, and he was shut in with his better thoughts and with God. His religious life rebloomed in wondrous beauty and sweetness. The blossoms of his early joy had fallen off, the storms had torn its branches and stripped it of its foliage, but its root had never perished, because he had never ceased to struggle for deliverance. Aspiration and hope live or die together in the human soul. The link that bound my friend to God was never wholly sundered. His better nature clung to the better way with a grasp that never let go altogether.

"O Doctor, I am a wonder to myself! It does seem to me that God has given back to me every good thing I possessed in the bright and blessed past. It has all come back to me. I see the light and feel the joy as I did when I first entered the new life. O it is wonderful! Doctor, God never gave me up, and I never ceased to yearn for his mercy and love, even in the darkest season of my unhappy life."

His very face had recovered its old look, and his voice its old tone. There could be no doubt of it—his soul had rebloomed in the life of God.

The last night came—they sent for me with the message,

"Come quickly! he is dying."

I found him with that look which I have seen on the faces of others who were nearing death—a radiance and a rapture that awed the beholder. O solemn, awful mystery of death! I have stood in its presence in every form of terror and of sweetness, and in every case the thought has been impressed upon me that it was a passage into the Great Realities.

"Doctor," he said, smiling, and holding my hand; "I had hoped to be with you in your office again, as in the old days—not as a business arrangement, but just to be with you, and revive old memories, and to live the old life over again. But that cannot be, and I must wait till we meet in the world of spirits, whither I go before you. It seems to be growing dark. I cannot see your face—hold my hand. I am going—going. I am on the waves—on the waves—." The radiance was still upon his face, but the hand I held no longer clasped mine—the wasted form was still. It was the end. (He was launched upon the Infinite Sea for the endless voyage.)

THE EMPEROR NORTON.

THAT was his title. He wore it with an air that was a strange mixture of the mock-heroic and the pathetic. He was mad on this one point, and strangely shrewd and well-informed on almost every other. Arrayed in a faded-blue uniform, with brass buttons and epaulettes, wearing a cocked-hat with an eagle's feather, and at times with a rusty sword at his side, he was a conspicuous figure in the streets of San Francisco, and a regular *habitué* of all its public places. In person he was stout, full-chested, though slightly stooped, with a large head heavily coated with bushy black hair, an aquiline nose, and dark gray eyes, whose mild expression added to the benignity of his face. On the end of his nose grew a tuft of long hairs, which he seemed to prize as a natural mark of royalty, or chieftainship. Indeed, there was a popular legend afloat that he was of true royal blood—a stray Bourbon, or something of the sort.

His speech was singularly fluent and elegant. The Emperor was one of the celebrities that no visitor failed to see. It is said that his mind was unhinged by a sudden loss of fortune in the early days, by the treachery of a partner in trade. The sudden blow was deadly, and the quiet, thrifty, affable man of business became a wreck. By nothing is the inmost quality of a man made more manifest than by the manner in which he meets misfortune. One, when the sky darkens, having strong impulse and weak will, rushes into suicide; another, with a large vein of cowardice, seeks to drown the sense of disaster in strong drink; yet another, tortured in every fiber of a sensitive organization, flees from the scene of his troubles and the faces of those that know him, preferring exile to shame. The truest man, when assailed by sudden calamity, rallies all the reserved forces of a splendid manhood to meet the shock, and, like a good ship, lifting itself from the trough of the swelling sea, mounts the wave and rides on. It was a curious idiosyncrasy that led this man, when fortune and reason were swept away at a stroke, to fall back upon this imaginary imperialism. The nature that could thus, when the real fabric of life was wrecked, construct such another by the exercise of a disordered imagination, must have been originally of a gentle and magnanimous type. The

broken fragments of mind, like those of a statue,
reveal the quality of the original creation. It may
be that he was happier than many who have worn
real crowns. Napoleon at Chiselhurst, or his
greater uncle at St. Helena, might have been gain-
er by exchanging lots with this man, who had the
inward joy of conscious greatness without its burden and its perils. To all public places he had
free access, and no pageant was complete without
his presence. From time to time he issued proclamations, signed "Norton I.," which the lively San
Francisco dailies were always ready to print con-
spicuously in their columns. The style of these
proclamations was stately, the royal first person
plural being used by him with all gravity and dignity. Ever and anon, as his uniform became di-
lapidated or ragged, a reminder of the condition
of the imperial wardrobe would be given in one or
more of the newspapers, and then in a few days he
would appear in a new suit. He had the *entrée* of
all the restaurants, and he lodged — nobody knew
where. It was said that he was cared for by members of the Freemason Society to which he belonged at the time of his fall. I saw him often
in my congregation in the Pine-street church, along
in 1858, and into the sixties. He was a respectful
and attentive listener to preaching. On the occasion of one of his first visits he spoke to me.

after the service, saying, in a kind and patronizing tone:

"I think it my duty to encourage religion and morality by showing myself at church, and to avoid jealousy I attend them all in turn."

He loved children, and would come into the Sunday-school, and sit delighted with their singing. When, in distributing the presents on a Christmas-tree, a necktie was handed him as the gift of the young ladies, he received it with much satisfaction, making a kingly bow of gracious acknowledgment. Meeting him one day, in the spring-time, holding my little girl by the hand, he paused, looked at the child's bright face, and taking a rose-bud from his button-hole, he presented it to her with a manner so graceful, and a smile so benignant, as to show that under the dingy blue uniform there beat the heart of a gentleman. He kept a keen eye on current events, and sometimes expressed his views with great sagacity. One day he stopped me on the street, saying:

"I have just read the report of the political sermon of Dr. —— (giving the name of a noted sensational preacher, who was in the habit, at times, of discussing politics from his pulpit). I disapprove political-preaching. What do you think?"

I expressed my cordial concurrence.

"I will put a stop to it. The preachers must stop preaching politics, or they must all come into one State Church. I will at once issue a decree to that effect."

For some unknown reason, that decree never was promulgated.

After the war, he took a deep interest in the reconstruction of the Southern States. I met him one day on Montgomery street, when he asked me in a tone and with a look of earnest solicitude:

"Do you hear any complaint or dissatisfaction concerning me from the South?"

I gravely answered in the negative.

"I was for keeping the country undivided, but I have the kindest feeling for the Southern people, and will see that they are protected in all their rights. Perhaps if I were to go among them in person, it might have a good effect. What do you think?"

I looked at him keenly as I made some suitable reply, but could see nothing in his expression but simple sincerity. He seemed to feel that he was indeed the father of his people. George Washington himself could not have adopted a more paternal tone.

Walking along the street behind the Emperor one day, my curiosity was a little excited by seeing him thrust his hand into the hip-pocket of his blue trousers with sudden energy. The hip-pocket, by the way, is a modern American stupidity, associated in the popular mind with rowdyism, pistol-shooting, and murder. Hip-pockets should be abolished wherever there are courts of law and civilized men and women. But what was the Emperor after? Withdrawing his hand just as I overtook him, the mystery was revealed—it grasped a thick Bologna sausage, which he began to eat with unroyal relish. It gave me a shock, but he was not the first royal personage who has exhibited low tastes and carnal hankerings.

He was seldom made sport of or treated rudely. I saw him on one occasion when a couple of passing hoodlums jeered at him. He turned and gave them a look so full of mingled dignity, pain, and surprise, that the low fellows were abashed, and uttering a forced laugh, with averted faces they hurried on. The presence that can bring shame to a San Francisco hoodlum must indeed be kingly, or in some way impressive. In that genus the beastliness and devilishness of American city-life reach their lowest denomination. When the brutality of the savage and the lowest forms of civilized vice are combined, human nature touches bottom.

The Emperor never spoke of his early life. The veil of mystery on this point increased the popular curiosity concerning him, and invested him with something of a romantic interest. There was one thing that excited his disgust and indignation. The Bohemians of the San Francisco press got into the practice of attaching his name to their satires and hits at current follies, knowing that the well-known "Norton I." at the end would insure a reading. This abuse of the liberty of the press he denounced with dignified severity, threatening extreme measures unless it were stopped. But nowhere on earth did the press exhibit more audacity, or take a wider range, and it would have required a sterner heart and a stronger hand than that of Norton I. to put a hook into its jaws.

The end of all human grandeur, real or imaginary, comes at last. The Emperor became thinner and more stooped as the years passed. The humor of his hallucination retired more and more into the background, and its pathetic side came out more strongly. His step was slow and feeble, and there was that look in his eyes so often seen in the old and sometimes in the young, just before the great change comes — a rapt, far-away look, suggesting that the invisible is coming into view, the shadows vanishing and the realities appearing. The familiar face and form were missed on the streets, and it was known that he was dead. He had gone to his lonely lodging, and quietly lain down and died. The newspapers spoke of him with pity and respect, and all San Francisco took time, in the midst of its roar-and-rush fever of perpetual excitement, to give a kind thought to the dead man who had passed over to the life where all delusions are laid aside, where the mystery of life shall be revealed, and where we shall see that through all its tangled web ran the golden thread of mercy. His life was an illusion, and the thousands who sleep with him in Lone Mountain waiting the judgment-day were his brothers.

CAMILLA CAIN.

SHE was from Baltimore, and had the fair face and gentle voice peculiar to most Baltimore women. Her organization was delicate but elastic—one of the sort that bends easily, but is hard to break. In her eyes was that look of wistful sadness so often seen in holy women of her type. Timid as a fawn, in the class-meeting she spoke of her love to Jesus and delight in his service in a voice low and a little hesitating, but with strangely thrilling effect. The meetings were sometimes held in her own little parlor in the cottage on Dupont street, and then we always felt that we had met where the Master himself was a constant and welcome guest. She was put into the crucible. For more than fifteen years she suffered unceasing and intense bodily pain. Imprisoned in her sick-chamber, she fought her long, hard battle. The pain-distorted limbs lost their use, the patient face waxed more wan, and the traces of agony were on it always; the soft, loving eyes were often tear-washed. The fires were hot, and they burned on through the long, long years without respite. The mystery of it all was too deep for me; it was too deep for her. But somehow it does seem that the highest suffer most:

The sign of rank in Nature
Is capacity for pain,
And the anguish of the singer
Makes the sweetness of the strain.

The victory of her faith was complete. If the inevitable *why?* sometimes was in her thought, no shadow of distrust ever fell upon her heart. Her sick-room was the quietest, brightest spot in all the city. How often did I go thither weary and faint with the roughness of the way, and leave feeling that I had heard the voices and inhaled the odors of paradise! A little talk, a psalm, and then a prayer, during which the room seemed to be filled .with angel-presences; after which the thin, pale face was radiant with the light reflected from our Immanuel's face. I often went to see her, not so much to convey as to get a blessing. Her heart was kept fresh as a rose of Sharon in the dew of the morning. The children loved to be near her; and the pathetic face of the dear crippled boy, the pet of the family, was always brighter in her presence. Thrice death came into the home-circle with

its shock and mighty wrenchings of the heart, but
the victory was not his, but hers. Neither death
nor life could separate her from the love of her
Lord. She was one of the elect. The elect are
those who know, having the witness in themselves
She was conqueror of both—life with its pain and
its weariness, death with its terror and its tragedy.
She did not endure merely, she triumphed. Borne
on the wings of a mighty faith, her soul was at
times lifted above all sin, and temptation, and pain,
and the sweet, abiding peace swelled into an ecstasy of sacred joy. Her swimming eyes and
rapt look told the unutterable secret. She has
crossed over the narrow stream on whose margin
she lingered so long; and there was joy on the other
side when the gentle, patient, holy Camilla Cain
joined the glorified throng.

> O though oft depressed and lonely,
>   All my fears are laid aside,
> If I but remember only
>   Such as these have lived and died!

6

LONE MOUNTAIN.

THE sea-wind sweeps over the spot at times in gusts like the frenzy of hopeless grief, and at times in sighs as gentle as those heaved by aged sorrow in sight of eternal rest. The voices of the great city come faintly over the sand-hills, with subdued murmur like a lullaby to the pale sleepers that are here lying low. When the winds are quiet, which is not often, the moan of the mighty Pacific can be heard day or night, as if it voiced in muffled tones the unceasing woe of a world under the reign of death. Westward, on the summit of a higher hill, a huge cross stretches its arms as if embracing the living and the dead—the first object that catches the eye of the weary voyager as he nears the Golden Gate, the last that meets his lingering gaze as he goes forth upon the great waters. O sacred emblem of the faith with which we launch upon life's stormy main—of the hope that assures that we shall reach

(82)

the port when the night and the tempest are past!
When the winds are high, the booming of the
breakers on the cliff sounds as if nature were im-
patient of the long, long delay, and had anticipated the last thunders that wake the sleeping
dead. On a clear day, the blue Pacific, stretching
away beyond the snowy surf-line, symbolizes the
shoreless sea that rolls through eternity. The
Cliff House road that runs hard by is the chief
drive of the pleasure-seekers of San Francisco.
Gayety, and laughter, and heart-break, and tears,
meet on the drive; the wail of agony and the
laugh of gladness mingle as the gay crowds dash
by the slow-moving procession on its way to the
grave. How often have I made that slow, sad journey to Lone Mountain — a *Via Doloroso* to many
who have never been the same after they had gone
thither, and coming back found the light quenched
and the music hushed in their homes! Thither the
dead Senator was borne, followed by the tramping
thousands, rank on rank, amid the booming of min-
ute-guns, the tolling of bells, the measured tread of
plumed soldiers, and the roll of drums. Thither
was carried, in his rude coffin, the "unknown
man" found dead in the streets, to be buried in
potter's-field. Thither was borne the hard and
grasping idolater of riches, who clung to his coin,
and clutched for more, until he was dragged away

by the one hand that was colder and stronger than his own. Here was brought the little child, out of whose narrow grave there blossomed the beginnings of a new life to the father and mother, who in the better life to come will be found among the blessed company of those whose only path to paradise lay through the valley of tears. Here were brought the many wanderers, whose last earthly wish was to go back home, on the other side of the mountains, to die, but were denied by the stern messenger who never waits nor spares. And here was brought the mortal part of the aged disciple of Jesus, in whose dying-chamber the two worlds met, and whose death-throes were demonstrably the birth of a child of God into the life of glory.

The first time I ever visited the place was to attend the funeral of a suicide. The dead man I had known in Virginia, when I was a boy. He was a graduate of the Virginia Military Institute, and when I first knew him he was the captain of a famous volunteer company. He was as handsome as a picture—the admiration of the girls, and the envy of the young men of his native town. He was among the first who rushed to California on the discovery of gold, and of all the heroic men who gave early California its best bias none was knightlier than this handsome Virginian;

none won stronger friends, or had brighter hopes. He was the first State Senator from San Francisco. He had the magnetism that won and the nobility that retained the love of men. Some men push themselves forward by force of intellect or of will —this man was pushed upward by his friends because he had their hearts. He married a beautiful woman, whom he loved literally unto death. I shall not recite the whole story. God only knows it fully, and he will judge righteously. There was trouble, rage, and tears, passionate partings and penitent reunions—the old story of love dying a lingering yet violent death. On the fatal morning I met him on Washington street. I noticed his manner was hurried and his look peculiar, as I gave him the usual salutation and a hearty grasp of the hand. As he moved away, I looked after him with mingled admiration and pity, until his faultless figure turned the corner and disappeared.

Ten minutes afterward he lay on the floor of his room dead, with a bullet through his brain, his hair dabbled in blood. At the funeral-service, in the little church on Pine street, strong men bowed their heads and sobbed. His wife sat on a front seat, pale as marble and as motionless, her lips compressed as with inward pain; but I saw no tears on the beautiful face. At the grave the body had been lowered to its resting-place, and all being ready, the attendants standing with uncovered heads, I was just about to begin the reading of the solemn words of the burial-service, when a tall, blue-eyed man with gray side-whiskers pushed his way to the head of the grave, and in a voice choked with passion, exclaimed:

"There lies as noble a gentleman as ever breathed, and he owes his death to that fiend!" pointing his finger at the wife, who stood pale and silent looking down into the grave.

She gave him a look that I shall never forget, and the large steely-blue eyes flashed fire, but she spoke no word. I spoke:

"Whatever may be your feelings, or whatever the occasion for them, you degrade yourself by such an exhibition of them *here*."

"That is so, sir; excuse me, my feelings overcame me," he said, and retiring a few steps, he leaned upon a branch of a scrub-oak and sobbed like a child.

The farce and the tragedy of real life were here exhibited on another occasion. Among my acquaintances in the city were a man and his wife who were singularly mismatched. He was a plain, unlettered, devout man, who in a prayer-meeting or class-meeting talked with a simple-hearted earnestness that always produced a happy effect.

She was a cultured woman, ambitious and worldly, and so fine-looking that in her youth she must have been a beauty and a belle. They lived in different worlds, and grew wider apart as time passed by—he giving himself to religion, she giving herself to the world. In the gay city circles in which she moved she was a little ashamed of the quiet, humble old man, and he did not feel at home among them. There was no formal separation, but it was known to the friends of the family that for months at a time they never lived together. The fashionable daughters went with their mother. The good old man, after a short sickness, died in great peace. I was sent for to officiate at the funeral-service. There was a large gathering of people, and a brave parade of all the externals of grief, but it was mostly dry-eyed grief, so far as I could see. At the grave, just as the sun that was sinking in the ocean threw his last rays upon the spot, and the first shovelful of earth fell upon the coffin that had been gently lowered to its resting-place, there was a piercing shriek from one of the carriages, followed by the exclamation:

"What shall I do? How can I live? I have lost my all! O! O! O!"

It was the dead man's wife. Significant glances and smiles were interchanged by the by-standers. Approaching the carriage in which the woman was sitting, I laid my hand upon her arm, looked her in the face, and said:

"Hush!"

She understood me, and not another sound did she utter. Poor woman! She was not perhaps as heartless as they thought she was. There was at least a little remorse in those forced exclamations, when she thought of the dead man in the coffin; but her eyes were dry, and she stopped very short.

Another incident recurs to me that points in a different direction. One day the most noted gambler in San Francisco called on me with the request that I should attend the funeral of one of his friends, who had died the night before. A splendid-looking fellow was this knight of the faro-table. More than six feet in height, with deep chest and perfectly rounded limbs, jet black hair, brilliant black eyes, clear olive complexion, and easy manners, he might have been taken for an Italian nobleman or a Spanish Don. He had a tinge of Cherokee blood in his veins. I have noticed that this cross of the white and Cherokee blood often results in producing this magnificent physical development. I have known a number of women of this lineage, who were very queens in their beauty and carriage. But this noted gambler was illiterate. The only book of which he knew or cared much was one that had fifty-two pages, with twelve pictures. If he had been educated, he might have handled the reins of government, instead of presiding over a nocturnal banking institution.

"Parson, can you come to number ——, on Kearney street, to-morrow at ten o'clock, and give us a few words and a prayer over a friend of mine, who died last night?"

I promised to be there, and he left.

His friend, like himself, had been a gambler. He was from New York. He was well educated, gentle in his manners, and a general favorite with the rough and desperate fellows with whom he associated, but with whom he seemed out of place. The passion for gambling had put its terrible spell on him, and he was helpless in its grasp. But though he mixed with the crowds that thronged the gambling-hells, he was one of them only in the absorbing passion for play. There was a certain respect shown him by all that venturesome fraternity. He went to Frazer River during the gold excitement. In consequence of exposure and privation in that wild chase after gold, which proved fatal to so many eager adventurers, he contracted pulmonary disease, and came back to San Francisco to die. He had not a dollar. His gambler friend took charge of him, placed him in a good boarding-place, hired a nurse for him, and for nearly a year provided for all his wants.

"I knew him when he was in better luck," said he, "and felt like I ought to stand by him."

At the funeral there was a large attendance of gamblers, with a sprinkling of women whose social *status* was not clearly defined to my mind. During the solemn service there was deep feeling. Down the bronzed face of the noted gambler the tears flowed freely, as he stood near the foot of the coffin. As he listened to those thrilling words from the fifteenth chapter of First Corinthians, there was a look of wonder, and inquiry, and awe on his face. What were his thoughts? At the cemetery they lowered the body tenderly into the grave, listened with uncovered heads to the closing words of the ritual for the burial of the dead, and then dispersed, doubtless going back to the old life, but it may be with some better thoughts.

I was sitting in my office at work on the same afternoon, when the tall and portly form of the gambler presented itself.

"Parson, you went through that funeral this morning in a way that suited me. Take this, with my thanks."

As he spoke he extended his hand with ever so many shining gold pieces—twenties, tens, and fives.

"No," I said; "it is contrary to the usage of my Church and to my own taste to take pay for burying a fellow-man."

After thoughtfully considering a moment, he said:

"That suits me. But would you object to wearing a little trinket on your watch-chain, coming from a man like me?"

Seeing his heart was set on it, I told him I would not decline taking such a token of his good-will. The gift of a most beautiful and costly Japanese crystal was the result. I wore it for many years, and when it was lost at Los Angeles, in 1877, I felt quite sorry. It reminded me of an incident that showed the good side of human nature in a circle in which the other side is usually uppermost.

My pencil lingers, as I think of this far-away resting-place of the dead, and as I lay it down, I seem to hear the ocean's moan and the dirge of the winds; and the pale images of many, many faces that have faded away into the darkness of death rise before me, some of them with radiant smiles and beckoning hands.

NEWTON.

THE miners called him the "Wandering Jew." That was behind his back. To his face they addressed him as Father Newton. He walked his circuits in the northern mines. No pedestrian could keep up with him, as with his long form bending forward, his immense yellow beard that reached to his breast floating in the wind, he strode from camp to camp with the message of salvation. It took a good trotting-horse to keep pace with him. Many a stout prospector, meeting him on a highway, after panting and straining to bear him company, had to fall behind, gazing after him in wonder, as he swept out of sight at that marvelous gait. There was a glitter in his eye, and an intensity of gaze that left you in doubt whether it was genius or madness that it bespoke. It was, in truth, a little of both. He had genius. Nobody ever talked with him, or heard him preach, without finding it out. The rough fellow who offended

him at a camp-meeting, near "Yankee Jim's," no
doubt thought him mad. He was making some
disturbance just as the long-bearded old preacher
was passing with a bucket of water in his hand.

"What do you mean?" he thundered, stopping
and fixing his keen eye upon the rowdy.

A rude and profane reply was made by the jeer-
ing sinner.

Quick as thought Newton rushed upon him with
flashing eye and uplifted bucket, a picture of fiery
wrath that was too much for the thoughtless scoffer, who fled in terror amid the laughter of the
crowd. The vanquished son of Belial had no
sympathy from anybody, and the plucky preacher
was none the less esteemed because he was ready
to defend his Master's cause with carnal weapons.
The early Californians left scarcely any path of
sin unexplored, and were a sad set of sinners, but
for virtuous women and religion they never lost
their reverence. Both were scarce in those days,
when it seemed to be thought that gold-digging
and the Decalogue could not be made to harmon-
ize. The pioneer preachers found that one good
woman made a better basis for evangelization than
a score of nomadic bachelors. The first accession
of a woman to a church in the mines was an
epoch in its history. The church in the house of
Lydia was the normal type—it must be anchored

to woman's faith, and tenderness, and love, in the home.

He visited San Francisco during my pastorate in 1858. On Sunday morning he preached a sermon of such extraordinary beauty and power that at the night-service the house was crowded by a curious congregation, drawn thither by the report of the forenoon effort. His subject was the faith of the mother of Moses, and he handled it in his own way. The powerful effect of one passage I shall never forget. It was a description of the mother's struggle, and the victory of her faith in the crisis of her trial. No longer able to protect her child, she resolves to commit him to her God. He drew a picture of her as she sat weaving together the grasses of the little ark of bulrushes, her hot tears falling upon her work, and pausing from time to time with her hand pressed upon her throbbing heart. At length, the little vessel is finished, and she goes by night to the bank of the Nile, to take the last chance to save her boy from the knife of the murderers. Approaching the river's edge, with the ark in her hands, she stoops a moment, but her mother's heart fails her. How can she give up her child? In frenzy of grief she sinks upon her knees, and lifting her gaze to the heavens, passionately prays to the God of Israel. That prayer! It was the wail of a breaking heart, a cry out of the depths of a mighty agony. But as she prays the inspiration of God enters her soul, her eyes kindle, and her face beams with the holy light of faith. She rises, lifts the little ark, looks upon the sleeping face of the fair boy, prints a long, long kiss upon his brow, and then with a firm step she bends down, and placing the tiny vessel upon the waters, lets it go. "And away it went," he said, "rocking upon the waves as it swept beyond the gaze of the mother's straining eyes. The monsters of the deep were there, the serpent of the Nile was there, behemoth was there, but the child slept as sweetly and as safely upon the rocking waters as if it were nestled upon its mother's breast—*for God was there!*" The effect was electric. The concluding words, "for God was there!" were uttered with upturned face and lifted hands, and in a tone of voice that thrilled the hearers like a sudden clap of thunder from a cloud over whose bosom the lightnings had rippled in gentle flashes. It was true eloquence.

In a revival-meeting, on another occasion, he said, in a sermon of terrific power: "O the hardness of the human heart! Yonder is a man in hell. He is told that there is one condition on which he may be delivered, and that is that he must get the consent of every good being in the universe. A ray of hope enters his soul, and he sets out to comply with the condition. He visits heaven and earth, and finds sympathy and consent from all. All the holy angels consent to his pardon; all the pure and holy on earth consent; God himself repeats the assurance of his willingness that he may be saved. Even in hell, the devils do not object, knowing that his misery only heightens theirs. All are willing, all are ready — all but *one* man. He refuses; he will not consent. A monster of cruelty and wickedness, he refuses his simple consent to save a soul from an eternal hell! Surely a good God and all good beings in the universe would turn in horror from such a monster. *Sinner, you are that man!* The blessed God, the Holy Trinity, every angel in heaven, every good man and woman on earth, are not only willing but anxious that you shall be saved. But you will not consent. You refuse to come to Jesus that you may have life. You are the murderer of your own immortal soul. You drag yourself down to hell. You lock the door of your own dungeon of eternal despair, and throw the key into the bottomless pit, by rejecting the Lord that bought you with his blood! You will be lost! you must be lost! you ought to be lost!"

The words were something like these, but the energy, the passion, the frenzy of the speaker must be imagined. Hard and stubborn hearts were moved under that thrilling appeal. They were made to feel that the preacher's picture of a self-doomed soul described their own cases. There was joy in heaven that night over repenting sinners.

This old man of the mountains was a walking encyclopedia of theological and other learning. He owned books that could not be duplicated in California; and he read them, digested their contents, and constantly surprised his cultivated hearers by the affluence of his knowledge, and the fertility of his literary and classic allusion. He wrote with elegance and force. His weak point was orthography. He would trip sometimes in the spelling of the most common words. His explanation of this weakness was curious: He was a printer in Mobile, Alabama. On one occasion a thirty-two-page book-form of small type was "pied." "I undertook," said he, "to set that pied form to rights, and, in doing so, the words got so mixed in my brain that my spelling was spoiled forever!"

He went to Oregon, and traveled and preached from the Cascade Mountains to Idaho, thrilling, melting, and amusing, in turn, the crowds that came out to hear the wild-looking man whose coming was so sudden, and whose going was so rapid, that they were lost in wonder, as if gazing at a meteor that flashed across the sky.

He was a Yankee from New Hampshire, who,

7

going to Alabama, lost his heart, and was ever afterward intensely Southern in all his convictions and affections. His fiery soul found congenial spirits among the generous, hot-blooded people of the Gulf States, whose very faults had a sort of charm for this impulsive, generous, erratic, gifted, man. He made his way back to his New England hills, where he is waiting for the sunset, often turning a longing eye southward, and now and then sending a greeting to Alabama.

THE CALIFORNIA POLITICIAN.

THE California politician of the early days was plucky. He had to be so, for faint heart won no votes in those rough times. One of the Marshalls (Tom or Ned—I forget which), at the beginning of a stump-speech one night in the mines, was interrupted by a storm of hisses and execrations from a turbulent crowd of fellows, many of whom were full of whisky. He paused a moment, drew himself up to his full height, coolly took a pistol from his pocket, laid it on the stand before him, and said:

"I have seen bigger crowds than this many a time. I want it to be fully understood that I came here to make a speech to-night, and I am going to do it, or else there will be a funeral or two."

That touch took with that crowd. The one thing they all believed in was courage. Marshall made one of his grandest speeches, and at the close the delighted miners bore him in triumph from the rostrum.

That was a curious exordium of "Uncle Peter Mehan," when he made his first stump-speech at Sonora: "Fellow-citizens, *I was born an orphin at a very early period of my life.*" He was a candidate for supervisor, and the good-natured miners elected him triumphantly. He made a good supervisor, which is another proof that book-learning and elegant rhetoric are not essential where there are integrity and native good sense. Uncle Peter never stole any thing, and he was usually on the right side of all questions that claimed the attention of the county-fathers of Tuolumne.

In the early days, the Virginians, New Yorkers, and Tennesseans, led in politics. Trained to the stump at home, the Virginians and Tennesseans were ready on all occasions to run a primary-meeting, a convention, or a canvass. There was scarcely a mining-camp in the State in which there was not a leading local politician from one or both of these States. The New Yorker understood all the inside management of party organization, and was up to all the smart tactics developed in the lively struggles of parties in the times when Whiggery and Democracy fiercely fought for rule in the Empire State. Broderick was a New Yorker, trained by Tammany in its palmy days. He was a chief,

who rose from the ranks, and ruled by force of
will. Thick-set, strong-limbed, full-chested, with
immense driving-power in his back-head, he was
an athlete whose stalwart *physique* was of more
value to him than the gift of eloquence, or even
the power of money. The sharpest lawyers and
the richest money-kings alike went down before
this uncultured and moneyless man, who domi-
nated the clans of San Francisco simply by right
of his manhood. He was not without a sort of
eloquence of his own. He spoke right to the point,
and his words fell like the thud of a shillalah, or
rang like the clash of steel. He dealt with the
rough elements of politics in an exciting and turbulent period of California politics, and was more
of a border chief than an Ivanhoe in his modes of
warfare. He reached the United States Senate,
and in his first speech in that august body he honored his manhood by an allusion to his father, a
stone-mason, whose hands, said Broderick, had
helped to erect the very walls of the chamber in
which he spoke. When a man gets as high as the
United States Senate, there is less tax upon his
magnanimity in acknowledging his humble origin
than while he is lower down the ladder. You seldom hear a man boast how low he began until
he is far up toward the summit of his ambition.
Ninety-nine out of every hundred self-made men

are at first more or less sensitive concerning their low birth; the hundredth man who is not is a man indeed.

Broderick's great rival was Gwin. The men were antipodes in every thing except that they belonged to the same party. Gwin still lives, the most colossal figure in the history of California. He looks the man he is. Of immense frame, ruddy complexion, deep-blue eyes that almost blaze when he is excited, rugged yet expressive features, a massive head crowned with a heavy suit of silver-white hair, he is marked by Nature for leadership. Common men seem dwarfed in his presence. After he had dropped out of California politics for awhile, a Sacramento hotel-keeper expressed what many felt during a legislative session: "I find myself looking around for Gwin. I miss the chief."

My first acquaintance with Dr. Gwin began with an incident that illustrates the man and the times. It was in 1856. The Legislature was in session at Sacramento, and a United States Senator was to be elected. I was making a tentative movement toward starting a Southern Methodist newspaper, and visited Sacramento on that business. My friend Major P. L. Solomon was there, and took a friendly interest in my enterprise. He proposed to introduce me to the leading men of both parties, and I thankfully availed myself of his courtesy.

Among the first to whom he presented me was a noted politician who, both before and since, has enjoyed a national notoriety, and who still lives, and is as ready as ever to talk or fight. His name I need not give. I presented to him my mission, and he seemed embarrassed.

"I am with you, of course. My mother was a Methodist, and all my sympathies are with the Methodist Church. I am a Southern man in all my convictions and impulses, and I am a Southern Methodist in principle. But you see, sir, I am a candidate for United States Senator, and sectional feeling is likely to enter into the contest, and if it were known that my name was on your list of subscribers, it might endanger my election."

He squeezed my arm, told me he loved me and my Church, said he would be happy to see me often, and so forth—but he did not give me his name. I left him, saying in my heart, Here is a politician.

Going on together, in the corridor we met Gwin. Solomon introduced me, and told him my business.

"I am glad to know that you are going to start a Southern Methodist newspaper. No Church can do without its organ. Put me down on your list, and come with me, and I will make all these fellows subscribe. There is not much religion among them, I fear, but we will make them take the paper."

This was said in a hearty and pleasant way, and he took me from man to man, until I had gotten more than a dozen names, among them two or three of his most active political opponents.

This incident exhibits the two types of the politician, and the two classes of men to be found in all communities—the one all "blarney" and self-ishness, the other with real manhood redeeming poor human nature, and saving it from utter contempt. The senatorial prize eluded the grasp of both aspirants, but the reader will not be at a loss to guess whose side I was on. Dr. Gwin made a friend that day, and never lost him. It was this sort of fidelity to friends that, when fortune frowned on the grand old Senator after the collapse at Appomattox, rallied thousands of true hearts to his side, among whom were those who had fought him in many a fierce political battle. Broderick and Gwin were both, by a curious turn of political fortune, elected by the same Legislature to the United States Senate. Broderick sleeps in Lone Mountain, and Gwin still treads the stage of his former glory, a living monument of the days when California politics was half romance and half tragedy. The friend and *protégé* of General Andrew Jackson, a member of the first Constitutional Convention of California, twice United States Senator, a prominent figure in the civil war, the father

of the great Pacific Railway, he is the front figure
on the canvas of California history.

Gwin was succeeded by McDougall. What a
man was he! His face was as classic as a Greek
statue. It spoke the student and the scholar in
every line. His hair was snow-white, his eyes
bluish-gray, and his form sinewy and elastic. He
went from Illinois, with Baker and other men of
genius, and soon won a high place at the bar of
San Francisco. I heard it said, by an eminent
jurist, that when McDougall had put his whole
strength into the examination of a case, his side
of it was exhausted. His reading was immense,
his learning solid. His election was doubtless a
surprise to himself as well as to the California
public. The day before he left for Washington
City, I met him in the street, and as we parted I
held his hand a moment, and said:

"Your friends will watch your career with hope
and with fear."

He knew what I meant, and said, quickly:

"I understand you. You are afraid that I
will yield to my weakness. for strong drink.
But you may be sure I will play the man, and
California shall have no cause to blush on my
account."

That was his fatal weakness. No one, looking
upon his pale, scholarly face, and noting his fault-

lessly neat apparel, and easy, graceful manners, would have thought of such a thing. Yet he was a—I falter in writing it—a drunkard. At times he drank deeply and madly. When half intoxicated he was almost as brilliant as Hamlet, and as rollicking as Falstaff. It was said that even when fully drunk his splendid intellect never entirely gave way.

"McDougall commands as much attention in the Senate when drunk as any other Senator does when sober," said a Congressman in Washington in 1866. It is said that his great speech on the question of "confiscation," at the beginning of the war, was delivered when he was in a state of semi-intoxication. Be that as it may, it exhausted the whole question, and settled the policy of the Government.

"No one will watch your senatorial career with more friendly interest than myself; and if you will abstain wholly from all strong drink, we shall all be proud of you, I know."

"Not a drop will I touch, my friend; and I'll make you proud of me."

He spoke feelingly, and I think there was a moisture about his eye as he pressed my hand and walked away.

I never saw him again. For the first few months he wrote to me often, and then his letters came at longer intervals, and then they ceased. And then the newspapers disclosed the shameful secret—California's brilliant Senator was a drunkard. The temptations of the Capital were too strong for him. He went down into the black waters a complete wreck. He returned to the old home of his boyhood in New Jersey to die. I learned that he was lucid and penitent at the last. They brought his body back to San Francisco to be buried, and when at his funeral the words "I know that my Redeemer liveth," in clear soprano, rang through the vaulted cathedral like a peal of triumph, I indulged the hope that the spirit of my gifted and fated friend had, through the mercy of the Friend of sinners, gone from his boyhood hills up to the hills of God.

The typical California politician was Coffroth. The "boys" fondly called him "Jim" Coffroth. There is no surer sign of popularity than a popular abbreviation of this sort, unless it is a pet nickname. Coffroth was from Pennsylvania, where he had gained an inkling of politics and general literature. He gravitated into California politics by the law of his nature. He was born for this, having what a friend calls the gift of popularity. His presence was magnetic; his laugh was contagious; his enthusiasm irresistible. Nobody ever thought of taking offense at Jim Coffroth. He could change his politics with impunity without losing a friend—he never had a personal enemy; but I believe he only made that experiment once. He went off with the Know-nothings in 1855, and was elected by them to the State Senate, and was called to preside over their State Convention. He hastened back to his old party associates, and at the first convention that met in his county on his return from the Legislature, he rose and told them how lonesome he had felt while astray from the old fold, how glad he was to get back, and how humble he felt, concluding by advising all his late supporters to do as he had done by taking "a straight chute" for the old party. He ended amid a storm of applause, was reïnstated at once, and was made President of the next Democratic State Convention. There he was in his glory. His tact and good humor were infinite, and he held those hundreds of excitable and explosive men in the hollow of his hand. He would dismiss a dangerous motion with a witticism so apt that the mover himself would join in the laugh, and give it up. His broad face in repose was that of a Quaker, at other times that of a Bacchus. There was a religious streak in this jolly partisan, and he published several poems that breathed the sweetest and loftiest religious sentiment. The newspapers were a little disposed to make a joke of these ebullitions of devotional feeling, but they now make the light that casts a gleam of brightness upon the background of his life. I take from an old volume of the *Christian Spectator* one of these poems as a literary curiosity. Every man lives two lives. The rollicking politician, "Jim Coffroth," every Californian knew; the author of these lines was another man by the same name:

AMID THE SILENCE OF THE NIGHT.

"Behold, he that keepeth Israel shall neither slumber nor sleep."
Psalm cxxi.

Amid the silence of the night,
   Amid its lonely hours and dreary,
When we close the aching sight,
   Musing sadly, lorn and weary,
Trusting that to-morrow's light
   May reveal a day more cheery;

Amid affliction's darker hour,
   When no hope beguiles our sadness,
When Death's hurtling tempests lower,
   And forever shroud our gladness,
While Grief's unrelenting power
   Goads our stricken hearts to madness;

When from friends beloved we're parted,
   And from scenes our spirits love,
And are driven, broken-hearted,
   O'er a heartless world to rove;
When the woes by which we've smarted,
   Vainly seek to melt or move;

When we trust and are deluded,
  When we love and are denied,
When the schemes o'er which we brooded
  Burst like mist on mountain's side,
And, from every hope excluded,
  We in dark despair abide;   ⁄

Then, and ever, God sustains us,
  He whose eye no slumber knows,
Who controls each throb that pains us,
  And in mercy sends our woes,
And by love severe constrains us
  To avoid eternal throes.

Happy he whose heart obeys him! ·
  Lost and ruined who disown!
O if idols e'er displace him,
  Tear them from his chosen throne!
May our lives and language praise him!
  May our hearts be his alone!

He took defeat with a good nature that robbed
it of its sting, and made his political opponents
half sorry for having beaten him. He was talked
of for Governor at one time, and he gave as a
reason why he would like the office that "a great
many of his friends were in the State-prison, and
he wanted to use the pardoning power in their behalf." This was a jest, of course, referring to the
fact that as a lawyer much of his practice was in
the criminal courts. He was never suspected of
treachery or dishonor in public or private life.

His very ambition was unselfish: he was always ready to sacrifice himself in a hopeless candidacy if he could thereby help his party or a friend.

His good nature was tested once while presiding over a party convention at Sonora for the nomination of candidates for legislative and county offices. Among the delegates was the eccentric John Vallew, whose mind was a singular compound of shrewdness and flightiness, and was stored with the most out-of-the-way scraps of learning, philosophy, and poetry. Some one proposed Vallew's name as a candidate for the Legislature. He rose to his feet with a clouded face, and in an angry voice said:

"Mr. President, I am surprised and mortified. I have lived in this county more than seven years, and I have never had any difficulty with my neighbors. I did not know that I had an enemy in the world. What have I done, that it should be proposed to send me to the Legislature? What reason has anybody to think I am that sort of a man? To think I should have come to this! To propose to send me to the Legislature, when it is a notorious fact that you have never sent a man thither from this county *who did not come back morally and pecuniarily ruined!*"

The crowd saw the point, and roared with laughter, Coffroth, who had served in the previous session, joining heartily in the merriment. Vallew was excused.

Coffroth grew fatter and jollier; his strong intellect struggled against increasing sensual tendencies. What the issue might have been, I know not. He died suddenly, and his destiny was transferred to another sphere. So there dropped out of California-life a partisan without bitterness, a satirist without malice, a wit without a sting, the jolliest, freest, readiest man that ever faced a California audience on the hustings—the typical politician of California.

OLD MAN LOWRY.

I HAD marked his expressive physiognomy among my hearers in the little church in Sonora for some weeks before he made himself known to me. As I learned afterward, he was weighing the young preacher in his critical balances. He had a shrewd Scotch face, in which there was a mingling of keenness, benignity, and humor. His age might be sixty, or it might be more. He was an old bachelor, and wide guesses are sometimes made as to the ages of that class of men. They may not live longer than married men, but they do not show the effects of life's wear and tear so early. He came to see us one evening. He fell in love with the mistress of the parsonage, just as he ought to have done, and we were charmed with the quaint old bachelor. There was a piquancy, a sharp flavor, in his talk that was delightful. His aphorisms often crystallized a neglected truth in a form all his own. He was an

8 (113)

original character. There was nothing common-
place about him. He had his own way of saying
and doing every thing.

Society in the mines was limited in that day,
and we felt that we had found a real *thesaurus* in
this old man of unique mold. His visits were refreshing to us, and his plain-spoken criticisms were
helpful to me.

He had left the Church because he did not
agree with the preachers on some points of Christian ethics, and because they used tobacco. But
he was unhappy on the outside, and finding that my
views and habits did not happen to cross his peculiar notions, he came back. His religious experience
was out of the common order. Bred a Calvinist,
of the good old Scotch-Presbyterian type, he had
swung away from that faith, and was in danger of
rushing into Universalism, or infidelity. That
once famous and much-read little book, "John
Nelson's Journal," fell into his hands, and changed
his whole life. It led him to Christ, and to the
Methodists. He was a true spiritual child of the
unflinching Yorkshire stone-cutter. Like him he
despised half-way measures, and like him he was
aggressive in thought and action. What he liked
he loved, what he disliked he hated. Calvinism
he abhorred, and he let no occasion pass for pouring
into it the hot shot of his scorn and wrath. One

night I preached from the text, *Should it be accord-ing to thy mind?*

"The first part of your sermon," he said to me as we passed out of the church, "distressed me greatly. For a full half hour you preached straight-out Calvinism, and I thought you had ruined every thing; but you had left a little slip-gap, and crawled out at the last."

His ideal of a minister of the gospel was Dr. Keener, whom he knew at New Orleans before coming to California. He was the first man I ever heard mention Dr. Keener's name for the episcopacy. There was much in common between them. If my eccentric California bachelor friend did not have as strong and cool a head, he had as brave and true a heart as the incisive and chival-rous Louisiana preacher, upon whose head the miter was placed by the suffrage of his brethren at Memphis in 1870.

He became very active as a worker in the Church. I made him class-leader, and there have been few in that office who brought to its sacred duties as much spiritual insight, candor, and ten-derness. At times his words flashed like diamonds, showing what the Bible can reveal to a solitary thinker who makes it his chief study day and night. When needful, he could apply caustic that burned to the very core of an error of opinion or of practice. He took a class in the Sunday-school, and his freshness, acuteness, humor, and deep knowledge of the Scriptures, made him far more than an ordinary teacher. A fine pocket Bible was offered as a prize to the scholar who should, in three months, memorize the greatest number of Scripture verses. The wisdom of such a contest is questionable to me now, but it was the fashion then, and I was too young and self-distrustful to set myself against the current in such matters. The contest was an exciting one — two boys, Robert A—— and Jonathan R——, and one girl, Annie P——, leading all the school. Jonathan suddenly fell behind, and was soon distanced by his two competitors. Lowry, who was his teacher, asked him what was the reason of his sudden breakdown. The boy blushed, and stammered out:

"I did n't want to beat Annie."

Robert won the prize, and the day came for its presentation. The house was full, and everybody was in a pleasant mood. After the prize had been presented in due form and with a little flourish, Lowry arose, and producing a costly Bible, in a few words telling how magnanimously and gallantly Jonathan had retired from the contest, presented it to the pleased and blushing boy. The boys and girls applauded California fashion, and the old man's face glowed with satisfaction. He had in him curiously mingled the elements of the Puritan and the Cavalier—the uncompromising persistency of the one, and the chivalrous impulse and open-handedness of the other.

The old man had too many crotchets and too much combativeness to be popular. He spared no opinion or habit he did not like. He struck every angle within reach of him. In the state of society then existing in the mines there were many things to vex his soul, and keep him on the war-path. The miners looked upon him as a brave, good man, just a little daft. He worked a mining-claim on Wood's Creek, north of town, and lived alone in a tiny cabin on the hill above. That was the smallest of cabins, looking like a mere box from the trail which wound through the flat below. Two little scrub-oaks stood near it, under which he sat and read his Bible in leisure moments. There, above the world, he could commune with his own heart and with God undisturbed, and look down upon a race he half pitied and half despised. From the spot the eye took in a vast sweep of hill and dale: Bald Mountain, the most striking object in the near background, and beyond its dark, rugged mass the snowy summits of the Sierras, rising one above another, like gigantic stair-steps, leading up to the throne of the Eternal. This lonely height suited Lowry's strangely compounded nature. As a cynic, he looked down with contempt upon the petty life that seethed and frothed in the camps below; as a saint, he looked forth upon the wonders of God's handiwork around and above him.

There was an intensity in all that he did. Passing his mining-claim on horseback one day, I paused to look at him in his work. Clad in a blue flannel mining-suit, he was digging as for life. The embankment of red dirt and gravel melted away rapidly before his vigorous strokes, and he seemed to feel a sort of fierce delight in his work. Pausing a moment, he looked up and saw me.

"You dig as if you were in a hurry," I said.

"Yes, I have been digging here three years. I have a notion that I have just so much of the earth to turn over before I am turned under," he replied with a sort of grim humor.

He was still there when we visited Sonora in 1857. He invited us out to dinner, and we went. By skillful circling around the hill, we reached the little cabin on the summit with horse and buggy. The old man had made preparations for his expected guests. The floor of the cabin had been swept, and its scanty store of furniture put to rights, and a dinner was cooking in and on the little stove. His lady-guest insisted on helping in the preparation of the dinner, but was allowed to do nothing further than to arrange the dishes on the primitive table, which was set out under one of the little oaks in the yard. It was a miner's feast— can-fruits, can-vegetables, can-oysters, can-pickles, can-every thing nearly, with tea distilled from the Asiatic leaf by a receipt of his own. It was a hot day, and from the cloudless heavens the sun flooded the earth with his glory, and the shimmer of the sunshine was in the still air. We tried to be cheerful, but there was a pathos about the affair that touched us. He felt it too. More than once there was a tear in his eye. At parting, he kissed little Paul, and gave us his hand in silence. As we drove down the hill, he stood gazing after us with a look fixed and sad. The picture is still before me—the lonely old man standing sad and silent, the little cabin, the rude dinner-service under the oak, and the overarching sky. That was our last meeting. The next will be on the Other Side.

SUICIDE IN CALIFORNIA.

A HALF protest rises within me as I begin this Sketch. The page almost turns crimson under my gaze, and shadowy forms come forth out of the darkness into which they wildly plunged out of life's misery into death's mystery. Ghostly lips cry out, "Leave us alone! Why call us back to a world where we lost all, and in quitting which we risked all? Disturb us not to gratify the cold curiosity of unfeeling strangers. We have passed on beyond human jurisdiction to the realities we dared to meet. Give us the pity and courtesy of your silence, O living brother, who didst escape the wreck!" The appeal is not without effect, and if I lift the shroud that covers the faces of these dead self-destroyed, it will be tenderly, pityingly. These simple Sketches of real California-life would be imperfect if this characteristic feature were entirely omitted; for California was (and is yet) the land of suicides. In a single year there were one hun-

dred and six in San Francisco alone. The whole
number of suicides in the State would, if the horror
of each case could be even imperfectly imagined,
appal even the dryest statistician of crime. The
causes for this prevalence of self-destruction are
to be sought in the peculiar conditions of the
country, and the habits of the people. California,
with all its beauty, grandeur, and riches, has been
to the many who have gone thither a land of great
expectations, but small results. This was specially
the case in the earlier period of its history, after
the discovery of gold and its settlement by "Americans," as we call ourselves, *par excellence.* Hurled
from the topmost height of extravagant hope to
the lowest deep of disappointment, the shock is
too great for reaction; the rope, razor, bullet, or
deadly drug, finishes the tragedy. Materialistic
infidelity in California is the avowed belief of
multitudes, and its subtle poison infects the minds
and unconsciously the actions of thousands who
recoil from the dark abyss that yawns at the feet
of its adherents with its fascination of horror.
Under some circumstances, suicide becomes logical
to a man who has neither hope nor dread of a
hereafter. Sins against the body, and especially
the nervous system, were prevalent; and days of
pain, sleepless nights, and weakened wills, were the
precursors of the tragedy that promised change,

if not rest. The devil gets men inside a fiery circle, made by their own sin and folly, from which
there seems to be no escape but by death, and they
will unbar its awful door with their own trembling
hands. There is another door of escape for the
worst and most wretched, and it is opened to the
penitent by the hand that was nailed to the rugged
cross. These crises do come, when the next step
must be death or life—penitence or perdition. Do
sane men and women ever commit suicide? Yes
—and, No. Yes, in the sense that they sometimes
do it with even pulse and steady nerves. No, in
the sense that there cannot be perfect soundness in
the brain and heart of one who violates a primal
instinct of human nature. Each case has its own
peculiar features, and must be left to the all-seeing
and all-pitying Father. Suicide, where it is not
the greatest of crimes, is the greatest of misfort-
unes. The righteous Judge will classify its victims.

A noted case in San Francisco was that of a
French Catholic priest. He was young, brilliant,
and popular—beloved by his flock, and admired
by a large circle outside. He had taken the solemn vows of his order in all sincerity of purpose,
and was distinguished as well for his zeal in his
pastoral work as for his genius. But temptation
met him, and he fell. It came in the shape in

which it assailed the young Hebrew in Potiphar's house, and in which it overcame the poet-king of Israel. He was seized with horror and remorse, though he had no accuser save that voice within, which cannot be hushed while the soul lives. He ceased to perform the sacred functions of his office, making some plausible pretext to his superiors, not daring to add sacrilege to mortal sin. Shutting himself in his chamber, he brooded over his crime; or, no longer able to endure the agony he felt, he would rush forth, and walk for hours over the sand-dunes, or along the sea-beach. But no answer of peace followed his prayers, and the voices of nature soothed him not. He thought his sin unpardonable—at least, he would not pardon himself. He was found one morning lying dead in his bed in a pool of blood. He had severed the jugular-vein with a razor, which was still clutched in his stiffened fingers. His handsome and classic face bore no trace of pain. A sealed letter, lying on the table, contained his confession · and his farewell.

Among the lawyers in one of the largest mining towns of California was H. B——. He was a native of Virginia, and an *alumnus* of its noble University. He was a scholar, a fine lawyer, handsome and manly in person and bearing, and had the gift of popularity. Though the youngest lawyer in the town, he took a front place at the bar at once. Over the heads of several older aspirants, he was elected county judge. There was no ebb in the tide of his general popularity, and he had qualities that won the warmest regard of his inner circle of special friends. But in this case, as in many others, success had its danger. Hard drinking was the rule in those days. Horace B—— had been one of the rare exceptions. There was a reason for this extra prudence. He had that peculiar susceptibility to alcoholic excitement which has been the ruin of so many gifted and noble men. He knew his weakness, and it is strange that he did not continue to guard against the danger that he so well understood. Strange? No; this infatuation is so common in every-day life that we cannot call it strange. There is some sort of fatal fascination that draws men with their eyes wide open into the very jaws of this hell of strong drink. The most brilliant physician in San Francisco, in the prime of his magnificent young manhood, died of *delirium tremens*, the victim of a self-inflicted disease, whose horrors no one knew or could picture so well as himself. Who says man is not a fallen, broken creature, and that there is not a devil at hand to tempt him? This devil, under the guise of sociability, false pride, or moral cowardice, tempted Horace B——, and he yielded.

Like tinder touched by flame, he blazed into drunkenness, and again and again the proud-spirited, manly, and cultured young lawyer and jurist was seen staggering along the streets, maudlin or mad with alcohol. When he had slept off his madness, his humiliation was intense, and he walked the streets with pallid face and downcast eyes. The coarser-grained men with whom he was thrown in contact had no conception of the mental tortures he suffered, and their rude jests stung him to the quick. He despised himself as a weakling and a coward, but he did not get more than a transient victory over his enemy. The spark had struck a sensitive organization, and the fire of hell, smothered for the time, would blaze out again. He was fast becoming a common drunkard, the accursed appetite growing stronger, and his will weakening in accordance with that terrible law by which man's physical and moral nature visits retribution on all who cross its path. During a term of the court over which he presided, he was taken home one night drunk. A pistol-shot was heard by persons in the vicinity some time before daybreak; but pistol-shots, at all hours of the night, were then too common to excite special attention. Horace B—— was found next morning lying on the floor with a bullet through his head. Many a stout, heavy-bearded man had wet eyes when the body of the ill-fated and brilliant young Virginian was let down into the grave, which had been dug for him on the hill overlooking the town from the south-east.

In the same town there was a portrait-painter, a quiet, pleasant fellow, with a good face and easy, gentlemanly ways. As an artist, he was not without merit, but his gift fell short of genius. He fell in love with a charming girl, the eldest daughter of a leading citizen. She could not return his passion. The enamored artist still loved, and hoped against hope, lingering near her like a moth around a candle. There was another and more favored suitor in the case, and the rejected lover had all his hopes killed at one blow by her marriage to his rival. He felt that without her life was not worth living. He resolved to kill himself, and swallowed the contents of a two-ounce bottle of laudanum. After he had done the rash deed, a reaction took place. He told what he had done, and a physician was sent for. Before the doctor's arrival, the deadly drug asserted its power, and this repentant suicide began to show signs of going into a sleep from which it was certain he would never awake.

"My God! What have I done?" he exclaimed in horror. "Do your best, boys, to keep me from going to sleep before the doctor gets here."

The doctor came quickly, and by the prompt and very vigorous use of the stomach-pump he was saved. I was sent for, and found the would-be suicide looking very weak, sick, silly, and sheepish. He got well, and went on making pictures; but the picture of the fair, sweet girl, for love of whom he came so near dying, never faded from his mind. His face always wore a sad look, and he lived the life of a recluse, but he never attempted suicide again—he had had enough of that.

"It always makes me shudder to look at that place," said a lady, as we passed an elegant cottage on the western side of Russian Hill, San Francisco.

"Why so? The place to me looks specially cheerful and attractive, with its graceful slope, its shrubbery, flowers, and thick greensward."

"Yes, it is a lovely place, but it has a history that it shocks me to think of. Do you see that tall pumping-apparatus, with water-tank on top, in the rear of the house?"

"Yes; what of it?"

"A woman hanged herself there a year ago. The family consisted of the husband and wife, and two bright, beautiful children. He was thrifty and prosperous, she was an excellent housekeeper, and the children were healthy and well-behaved. In appearance a happier family could not be found on the hill. One day Mr. P—— came home at the usual hour, and, missing the wife's customary greeting, he asked the children where she was. The children had not seen their mother for two or three hours, and looked startled when they found she was missing. Messengers were sent to the nearest neighbors to make inquiries, but no one had seen her. Mr. P——'s face began to wear a troubled look as he walked the floor, from time to time going to the door and casting anxious glances about the premises.

About dusk a sudden shriek was heard, issuing from the water-tank in the yard, and the Irish servant-girl came rushing from it, with eyes distended and face pale with terror.

"Holy Mother of God! It's the Missus that's hanged herself!"

The alarm spread, and soon a crowd, curious and sympathetic, had collected. They found the poor lady suspended by the neck from a beam at the head of the staircase leading to the top of the inclosure. She was quite dead, and a horrible sight to see. At the inquest no facts were developed throwing any light on the tragedy. There had been no cloud in the sky portending the lightning-stroke that laid the happy little home in ruins. The husband testified that she was as bright and happy the morning of the suicide as he had ever seen her, and had parted with him at the door with the usual kiss. Every thing about the house that day bore the marks of her deft and skillful touch. The two children were dressed with accustomed neatness and good taste. And yet the bolt was in the cloud, and it fell before the sun had set! What was the mystery? Ever afterward I felt something of the feeling expressed by my lady friend when, in passing, I looked upon the structure which had been the scene of this singular tragedy.

One of the most energetic business men living in one of the foot-hill towns, on the northern edge of the Sacramento Valley, had a charming wife, whom he loved with a deep and tender devotion. As in all true love-matches, the passion of youth had ripened into a yet stronger and purer love with the lapse of years and participation in the joys and sorrows of wedded life. Their union had been blessed with five children, all intelligent, sweet, and full of promise. It was a very affectionate and happy household. Both parents possessed considerable literary taste and culture, and the best books and current magazine literature were read, discussed, and enjoyed in that quiet and elegant home amid the roses and evergreens. It was a little paradise in the hills, where Love, the home-angel, brightened every room and blessed

9

every heart. But trouble came in the shape of business reverses, and the worried look and wakeful nights of the husband told how heavy were the blows that had fallen upon this hard and willing worker. The course of ruin in California was fearfully rapid in those days. When a man's financial supports began to give way, they went with a crash. The movement downward was with a rush that gave no time for putting on the brakes. You were at the bottom, a wreck, almost before you knew it. So it was in this case. Every thing was swept away, a mountain of unpaid debts was piled up, credit was gone, clamor of creditors deafened him, and the gaunt wolf of actual want looked in through the door of the cottage upon the dear wife and little ones. Another shadow, and a yet darker one, settled upon them. The unhappy man had been tampering with the delusion of spiritualism, and his wife had been drawn with him into a partial belief in its vagaries. In their troubles they sought the aid of the "familiar spirits" that peeped and muttered through speaking, writing, and rapping mediums. This kept them in a state of morbid excitement that increased from day to day until they were wrought up to a tension that verged on insanity. The lying spirits, or the frenzy of his own heated brain, turned his thought to death as the only escape from want.

"I see our way out of these troubles, wife," he said one night, as they sat hand in hand in the bed-chamber, where the children were lying asleep. "We will all die together! This has been re-vealed to me as the solution of all our difficulties. Yes, we will enter the beautiful spirit-world to-gether! This is freedom! It is only getting out of prison. Bright spirits beckon and call us. I am ready."

There was a gleam of madness in his eyes, and, as he took a pistol from a bureau-drawer, an an-swering gleam flashed forth from the eyes of the wife, as she said:

"Yes, love, we will all go together. I too am ready."

The sleeping children were breathing sweetly, unmindful of the horror that the devil was hatch-ing.

"The children first, then you, and then me," he said, his eye kindling with increasing excite-ment.

He penciled a short note addressed to one of his old friends, asking him to attend to the burial of the bodies, then they kissed each of the sleeping children, and then—but let the curtain fall on the scene that followed. The seven were found next day lying dead, a bullet through the brain of each, the murderer, by the side of the wife, still holding the weapon of death in his hand, its muzzle against his right temple.

Other pictures of real life and death crowd upon my mind, among them noble forms and faces that were near and dear to me; but again I hear the appealing voices. The page before me is wet with tears—I cannot see to write.

FATHER FISHER.

HE came to California in 1855. The Pacific Conference was in session at Sacramento. It was announced that the new preacher from Texas would preach at night. The boat was detained in some way, and he just had time to reach the church, where a large and expectant congregation were in waiting. Below medium height, plainly dressed, and with a sort of peculiar shuffling movement as he went down the aisle, he attracted no special notice except for the profoundly reverential manner that never left him anywhere. But the moment he faced his audience and spoke, it was evident to them that a man of mark stood before them. They were magnetized at once, and every eye was fixed upon the strong yet benignant face, the capacious blue eyes, the ample forehead, and massive head, bald on top, with silver locks on either side. His tones in reading the Scripture and the hymns were unspeakably solemn and very

(133)

musical. The blazing fervor of the prayer that followed was absolutely startling to some of the preachers, who had cooled down under the depressing influence of the moral atmosphere of the country. It almost seemed as if we could hear the rush of the pentecostal wind, and see the tongues of flame. The very house seemed to be rocking on its foundations. By the time the prayer had ended, all were in a glow, and ready for the sermon. The text I do not now call to mind, but the impression made by the sermon remains. I had seen and heard preachers who glowed in the pulpit—this man burned. His words poured forth in a molten flood, his face shone like a furnace heated from within, his large blue eyes flashed with the lightning of impassioned sentiment, and anon swam in pathetic appeal that no heart could resist. Body, brain, and spirit, all seemed to feel the mighty afflatus. His very frame seemed to expand, and the little man who had gone into the pulpit with shuffling step and downcast eyes was transfigured before us. When, with radiant face, upturned eyes, an upward sweep of his arm, and trumpet-voice, he shouted, "Halleluiah to God!" the tide of emotion broke over all barriers, the people rose to their feet, and the church reëchoed with their responsive halleluiahs. The new preacher from Texas that night gave some Californians a new idea of evangelical eloquence, and took his place as a burning and a shining light among the ministers of God on the Pacific Coast.

"He is the man we want for San Francisco!" exclaimed the impulsive B. T. Crouch, who had kindled into a generous enthusiasm under that marvelous discourse.

He was sent to San Francisco. He was one of a company of preachers who have successively had charge of the Southern Methodist Church in that wondrous city inside the Golden Gate—Boring, Evans, Fisher, Fitzgerald, Gober, Brown, Bailey, Wood, Miller, Ball, Hoss, Chamberlin, Mahon, Tuggle, Simmons, Henderson. There was an almost unlimited diversity of temperament, culture, and gifts among these men; but they all had a similar experience in this, that San Francisco gave them new revelations of human nature and of themselves. Some went away crippled and scarred, some sad, some broken; but perhaps in the Great Day it may be found that for each and all there was a hidden blessing in the heart-throes of a service that seemed to demand that they should sow in bitter tears, and know no joyful reaping this side of the grave. O my brothers, who have felt the fires of that furnace heated seven times hotter than usual, shall we not in the resting-place beyond the river realize that these fires burned out of us the dross that we did not know was in our souls? The bird that comes out of the tempest with broken wing may henceforth take a lowlier flight, but will be safer because it ventures no more into the region of storms.

Fisher did not succeed in San Francisco, because he could not get a hearing. A little handful would meet him on Sunday mornings in one of the upper-rooms of the old City Hall, and listen to sermons that sent them away in a religious glow, but he had no leverage for getting at the masses. He was no adept in the methods by which the modern sensational preacher compels the attention of the novelty-loving crowds in our cities. An evangelist in every fiber of his being, he chafed under the limitations of his charge in San Francisco, and from time to time he would make a dash into the country, where, at camp-meetings and on other special occasions, he preached the gospel with a power that broke many a sinner's heart, and with a persuasiveness that brought many a wanderer back to the Good Shepherd's fold. His bodily energy, like his religious zeal, was unflagging. It seemed little less than a miracle that he could, day after day, make such vast expenditure of nervous energy without exhaustion. He put all his strength into every sermon and exhortation, whether addressed to admiring and weeping thousands at a great camp-meeting, or to a dozen or less "stand-bys" at the Saturday-morning service of a quar-terly-meeting.

He had his trials and crosses. Those who knew him intimately learned to expect his mightiest pul-pit efforts when the shadow on his face and the unconscious sigh showed that he was passing through the waters and crying to God out of the depths. In such experiences, the strong man is revealed and gathers new strength; the weak one goes under. But his strength was more than mere natural force of will, it was the strength of a mighty faith in God—that unseen force by which the saints work righteousness, subdue kingdoms, escape the violence of fire, and stop the mouths of lions.

As a flame of fire, Fisher itinerated all over Cal-ifornia and Oregon, kindling a blaze of revival in almost every place he touched. He was mighty in the Scriptures, and seemed to know the Book by heart. His was no rose-water theology. He be-lieved in a hell, and pictured it in Bible language with a vividness and awfulness that thrilled the stoutest sinner's heart; he believed in heaven, and spoke of it in such a way that it seemed that with him faith had already changed to sight. The gates of· pearl, the crystal river, the shining ranks of the white-robed throngs, their songs swelling as the sound of many waters, the holy love and rapture of the glorified hosts of the redeemed, were made to pass in panoramic procession before the listening multitudes, until the heaven he pictured seemed to be a present reality. He lived in the atmosphere of the supernatural; the spirit-world was to him most real.

"I have been out of the body," he said to me one day. The words were spoken softly, and his countenance, always grave in its aspect, deepened in its solemnity of expression as he spoke.

"How was that?" I inquired.

"It was in Texas. I was returning from a quarterly-meeting where I had preached one Sunday morning with great liberty and with unusual effect. The horses attached to my vehicle became frightened, and ran away. They were wholly beyond control, plunging down the road at a fearful speed, when, by a slight turn to one side, the wheel struck a large log. There was a concussion, and then a blank. The next thing I knew I was floating in the air above the road. I saw every thing as plainly as I see your face at this moment. There lay my body in the road, there lay the log, and there were the trees, the fence, the fields, and every thing, perfectly natural. My motion, which had been upward, was arrested, and as, poised in the air, I looked at my body lying there in the road so still, I felt a strong desire to go back to it, and found myself sinking toward it. The next thing I knew I was lying in the road where I had been thrown out, with a number of friends about me, some holding up my head, others chafing my hands, or looking on with pity or alarm. Yes, I was out of the body for a little, and I know there is a spirit-world."

His voice had sunk into a sort of whisper, and the tears were in his eyes. I was strangely thrilled. Both of us were silent for a time, as if we heard the echoes of voices, and saw the beckonings of shadowy hands from that Other World which sometimes seems so far away, and yet is so near to each one of us.

> Surely yon heaven, where angels see God's face,
>   Is not so distant as we deem
> From this low earth. 'T is but a little space,
>   'T is but a veil the winds might blow aside;
>   Yes, this all that us of earth divide
>   From the bright dwellings of the glorified,
>   The land of which I dream.

But it was no dream to this man of mighty faith, the windows of whose soul opened at all times Godward. To him immortality was a demonstrated fact, an experience. He had been out of the body.

Intensity was his dominating quality. He wrote

verses, and whatever they may have lacked of the subtle element that marks poetical genius, they were full of his ardent personality and devotional *abandon*. He compounded medicines whose virtues, backed by his own unwavering faith, wrought wondrous cures. On several occasions he accepted challenge to polemic battle, and his opponents found in him a fearless warrior, whose onset was next to irresistible. In these discussions it was no uncommon thing for his arguments to close with such bursts of spiritual power that the doctrinal duel would end in a great religious excitement, bearing disputants and hearers away on mighty tides of feeling that none could resist.

I saw in the *Texas Christian Advocate* an incident, related by Dr. F. A. Mood, that gives a good idea of what Fisher's eloquence was when in full tide:

"About ten years ago," says Dr. M., "when the train from Houston, on the Central Railroad, on one occasion reached Hempstead, it was peremptorily brought to a halt. There was a strike.among the *employés* of the road, on what was significantly called by the strikers 'The Death-warrant.' The road, it seems, had required all of their *employés* to sign a paper renouncing all claims to moneyed reparation in case of their bodily injury while in the service of the road. The excitement incident

to a strike was at its height at Hempstead when
our train reached there. The tracks were blocked
with trains that had been stopped as they arrived
from the different branches of the road, and the
employés were gathered about in groups, discussing
the situation—the passengers peering around with
hopeless curiosity. When our train stopped, the
conductor told us that we would have to lie over
all night, and many of the passengers left to find
accommodations in the hotels of the town. It was
now night, when a man came into the car and exclaimed, 'The strikers are tarring and feathering
a poor wretch out here, who has taken sides with
the road—come out and see it!' Nearly every one
in the car hastened out. I had risen, when a gentleman behind me gently pulled my coat, and said
to me, 'Sit down a moment.' He went on to say:
'I judge, sir, you are a clergyman; and I advise
you to remain here. You may be put to much in-
convenience by having to appear as a witness; in
a mob of that sort, too, there is no telling what
may follow.' I thanked him, and resumed my
seat. He then asked me to what denomination I
belonged, and upon my telling him I was a Methodist preacher, he asked eagerly and promptly if I
had ever met a Methodist preacher in Texas by
the name of Fisher, describing accurately the appearance of our glorified brother. Upon my tell-

ing him I knew him well, he proceeded to give the following incident. I give it as nearly as I can in his own words. Said he:

"'I am a Californian, have practiced law for years in that State, and, at the time I allude to, was district judge. I was holding court at —— [I can not now recall the name of the town he mentioned] and on Saturday was told that a Methodist camp meeting was being held a few miles from town. I determined to visit it, and reached the place of meeting in good time to hear the great preacher of the occasion—Father Fisher. The meeting was held in a river cañon. The rocks towered hundreds of feet on either side, rising over like an arch. Through the ample space over which the rocks hung the river flowed, furnishing abundance of cool water, while a pleasant breeze fanned a shaded spot. A great multitude had assembled—hundreds of very hard cases, who had gathered there, like myself, for the mere novelty of the thing. I am not a religious man—never have been thrown under religious influences. I respect religion, and respect its teachers, but have been very little in contact with religious things. At the appointed time, the preacher rose. He was small, with white hair combed back from his fore head, and he wore a venerable beard. I do not know much about the Bible, and I cannot quote

from his text, but he preached on the Judgment.
I tell you, sir, I have heard eloquence at the bar
and on the hustings, but I never heard such eloquence as that old preacher gave us that day. At
the last, when he described the multitudes calling
on the rocks and mountains to fall on them, I instinctively looked up to the arching rocks above
me. Will you believe it, sir?—as I looked up, to
my horror I saw the walls of the *cañon* swaying
as if they were coming together! Just then the
preacher called on all that needed mercy to kneel
down. I recollect he said something like this:
"'Every knee shall bow, and every tongue shall
confess;' and you might as well do it now as then."
The whole multitude fell on their knees—every
one of them. Although I had never done so before, I confess to you, sir, I got down on my knees.
I did not want to be buried right then and there
by those rocks that seemed to be swaying to de-
stroy me. The old man prayed for us; it was a
wonderful prayer! I want to see him once more;
where will I be likely to find him?'

"When he had closed his narrative, I said to
him: 'Judge, I hope you have bowed frequently
since that day.' 'Alas! no, sir,' he replied; 'not
much; but depend upon it, Father Fisher is a
wonderful orator—he made me think that day that
the walls of the *cañon* were falling.'"

He went back to Texas, the scene of his early labors and triumphs, to die. His evening sky was not cloudless—he suffered much—but his sunset was calm and bright; his waking in the Morning Land was glorious. If it was at that short period of silence spoken of in the Apocalypse, we may be sure it was broken when Fisher went in.

JACK WHITE.

THE only thing white about him was his name. He was a Piute Indian, and Piutes are neither white nor pretty. There is only one being in human shape uglier than a Piute "buck"—and that is a Piute squaw. One I saw at the Sink of the Humboldt haunts me yet. Her hideous face, begrimed with dirt and smeared with yellow paint, bleared and leering eyes, and horrid long, flapping breasts—ugh! it was a sight to make one feel sick. A degraded woman is the saddest spectacle on earth. Shakespeare knew what he was doing when he made the witches in Macbeth of the feminine gender. But as you look at them you almost forget that these Piute hags are women—they seem a cross between brute and devil. The unity of the human race is a fact which I accept; but some of our brothers and sisters are far gone from original loveliness. If Eve could see these Piute women, she would not be in a hurry to claim them as her

10   (145)

daughters; and Adam would feel like disowning some of his sons. As it appears to me, however, these repulsive savages furnish an argument in support of two fundamental facts of Christianity. One fact is, God did indeed make of one blood all the nations of the earth; the other is the fact of the fall and depravity of the human race. This unspeakable ugliness of these Indians is owing to their evil living. Dirty as they are, the little Indian children are not at all repulsive in expression. A boy of ten years, who stood half-naked, shivering in the wind, with his bow and arrows, had well-shaped features and a pleasant expression of countenance, with just a little of the look of animal cunning that belongs to all wild tribes. The ugliness grows on these Indians fearfully fast when it sets in. The brutalities of the lives they lead stamp themselves on their faces; and no other animal on earth equals in ugliness the animal called man, when he is nothing but an animal.

There was a mystery about Jack White's early life. He was born in the sage-brush desert beyond the Sierras, and, like all Indian babies, doubtless had a hard time at the outset. A Christian's pig or puppy is as well cared for as a Piute papoose. Jack was found in a deserted Indian camp in the mountains. He had been left to die, and was taken charge of by the kind-hearted John M.

White, who was then digging for gold in the Northern mines. He and his good Christian wife had mercy on the little Indian boy that looked up at them so pitifully with his wondering black eyes. At first he had the frightened and bewildered look of a captured wild creature, but he soon began to be more at ease. He acquired the English language slowly, and never did lose the peculiar accent of his tribe. The miners called him Jack White, not knowing any other name for him.

Moving to the beautiful San Ramon Valley, not far from the Bay of San Francisco, the Whites took Jack with them. They taught him the leading doctrines and facts of the Bible, and made him useful in domestic service. He grew and thrived. Broad-shouldered, muscular, and straight as an arrow, Jack was admired for his strength and agility by the white boys with whom he was brought into contact. Though not quarrelsome, he had a steady courage that, backed by his great strength, inspired respect and insured good treatment from them. Growing up amid these influences, his features were softened into a civilized expression, and his tawny face was not unpleasing. The heavy under-jaw and square forehead gave him an appearance of hardness which was greatly relieved by the honest look out of his eyes, and the smile which now and then would slowly creep over his face, like the movement of the shadow of a thin cloud on a calm day in summer. An Indian smiles deliberately, and in a dignified way—at least Jack did.

I first knew Jack at Santa Rosa, of which beautiful town his patron, Mr. White, was then the marshal. Jack came to my Sunday-school, and was taken into a class of about twenty boys taught by myself. They were the noisy element of the school, ranging from ten to fifteen years of age— too large to show the docility of the little lads, but not old enough to have attained the self-command and self-respect that come later in life. Though he was much older than any of them, and heavier than his teacher, this class suited Jack. The white boys all liked him, and he liked me. We had grand times with that class. The only way to keep them in order was to keep them very busy. The plan of having them answer in concert was adopted with decided results. It kept them awake—and the whole school with them, for California boys have strong lungs. Twenty boys speaking all at once, with eager excitement and flashing eyes, waked the drowsiest drone in the room. A gentle hint was given now and then to take a little lower key. In these lessons, Jack's deep guttural tones came in with marked effect, and it was delightful to see how he enjoyed it all. And the singing made his swarthy features glow with pleasure, though he rarely joined in it, having some misgiving as to the melody of his voice.

The truths of the gospel took strong hold of Jack's mind, and his inquiries indicated a deep interest in the matter of religion. I was therefore not surprised when, during a protracted-meeting in the town, Jack became one of the converts; but there was surprise and delight among the brethren at the class-meeting when Jack rose in his place and told what great things the Lord had done for him, dwelling with special emphasis on the words, "I am happy, because I know Jesus takes my sins away—I know he takes my sins away." His voice melted into softness, and a tear trickled down his cheek as he spoke; and when Dan Duncan, the leader, crossed over the room and grasped his hand in a burst of joy, there was a glad chorus of rejoicing Methodists over Jack White, the Piute convert.

Jack never missed a service at the church, and in the social-meetings he never failed to tell the story of his new-born joy and hope, and always with thrilling effect, as he repeated with trembling voice, "I am happy, because I know Jesus takes my sins away." Sin was a reality with Jack, and the pardon of sin the most wonderful of all facts. He never tired of telling it; it opened a new world

to him, a world of light and joy. Jack White in
the class-meeting or prayer-meeting, with beaming
face, and moistened eyes, and softened voice, telling of the love of Jesus, seemed almost of a different race from the wretched Piutes of the Sierras
and sage-brush.

Jack's baptism was a great event. It was by
immersion, the first baptism of the kind I ever
performed—and almost the last. Jack had been
talked to on the subject by some zealous brethren
of another "persuasion," who magnified that mode,
and though he was willing to do as I advised in
the matter, he was evidently a little inclined to the
more spectacular way of receiving the ordinance.
Mrs. White suggested that it might save future
trouble, and "spike a gun." So Jack, with four
others, was taken down to Santa Rosa Creek, that
went rippling and sparkling along the southern
edge of the town, and duly baptized in the name of
the Father, and of the Son, and of the Holy Ghost.
A great crowd covered the bridge just below, and
the banks of the stream; and when Wesley Mock,
the Asaph of Santa Rosa Methodism, struck up

> O happy day that fixed my choice
> On thee, my Saviour and my God,

and the chorus—

Happy day, happy day, when Jesus washed my sins away,

was swelled by hundreds of voices, it was a glad moment for Jack White and all of us. Religiously it was a warm time; but the water was very cold, it being one of the chilliest days I ever felt in that genial climate.

"You were rather awkward, Brother Fitzgerald, in immersing those persons," said my stalwart friend, Elder John McCorkle, of the "Christian" or Campbellite Church, who had critically but not unkindly watched the proceedings from the bridge. "If you will send for me the next time, I will do it for you," he added, pleasantly.

I fear it was awkwardly done, for the water was very cold, and a shivering man cannot be very graceful in his movements. I would have done better in a baptistery, with warm water and a rubber suit. But of all the persons I have welcomed into the Church during my ministry, the reception of no one has given me more joy than that of Jack White, the Piute Indian.

Jack's heart yearned for his own people. He wanted to tell them of Jesus, who could take away their sins; and perhaps his Indian instinct made him long for the freedom of the hills.

"I am going to my people," he said to me; "I want to tell them of Jesus. You will pray for me?" he added, with a quiver in his voice and a heaving chest.

He went away, and I have never seen him since. Where he is now, I know not. I trust I may meet him on Mount Sion, with the harpers harping with their harps, and singing, as it were, a new song before the throne.

Postscript.—Since this Sketch was penciled, the Rev. C. Y. Rankin, in a note dated Santa Rosa, California, August 3, 1880, says: "Mrs. White asked me to send you word of the peaceful death of Jack White (Indian). He died trusting in Jesus."

THE RABBI.

SEATED in his library, enveloped in a faded figured gown, a black velvet cap on his massive head, there was an Oriental look about him that arrested your attention at once. Power and gentleness, child-like simplicity, and scholarliness, were curiously mingled in this man. His library was a reflex of its owner. In it were books that the great public libraries of the world could not match —black-letter folios that were almost as old as the printing art, illuminated volumes that were once the pride and joy of men who had been in their graves many generations, rabbinical lore, theology, magic, and great volumes of Hebrew literature that looked, when placed beside a modern book, like an old ducal palace along-side a gingerbread cottage of to-day. I do not think he ever felt at home amid the hurry and rush of San Francisco. He could not adjust himself to the people. He was devout, and they were intensely worldly. Ho thundered this sentence from the teacher's desk in the synagogue one morning: "O ye Jews of San Francisco, you have so fully given yourselves up to material things that you are losing the very instinct of immortality. Your only idea of religion is to acquire the Hebrew language, *and you do n't know that!*" His port and voice were like those of one of the old Hebrew prophets. Elijah himself was not more fearless. Yet, how deep was his love for his race! Jeremiah was not more tender when he wept for the slain of the daughter of his people. His reproofs were resented, and he had a taste of persecution; but the Jews of San Francisco understood him at last. The poor and the little children knew him from the start. He lived mostly among his books, and in his school for poor children, whom he taught without charge. His habits were so simple and his bodily wants so few that it cost him but a trifle to live. When the synagogue frowned on him, he was as independent as Elijah at the brook Cherith. It is hard to starve a man to whom crackers and water are a royal feast.

His belief in God and in the supernatural was startlingly vivid. The Voice that spoke from Sinai was still audible to him, and the Arm that delivered Israel he saw still stretched out over the nations. The miracles of the Old Testament were as real to him as the premiership of Disraeli, or the financiering of the Rothschilds. There was, at the same time, a vein of rationalism that ran through his thought and speech. We were speaking one day on the subject of miracles, and, with his usual energy of manner, he said:

"There was no need of any literal angel to shut the mouths of the lions to save Daniel; *the awful holiness of the prophet was enough.* There was so much of God in him that the savage creatures submitted to him as they did to unsinning Adam. Man's dominion over nature was broken by sin, but in the golden age to come it will be restored. A man in full communion with God wields a divine power in every sphere that he touches."

His face glowed as he spoke, and his voice was subdued into a solemnity of tone that told how his reverent and adoring soul was thrilled with this vision of the coming glory of redeemed humanity.

He knew the New Testament by heart, as well as the Old. The sayings of Jesus were often on his lips.

One day, in a musing, half-soliloquizing way, I heard him say:

"It is wonderful, wonderful! a Hebrew peasant from the hills of Galilee, without learning, noble birth, or power, subverts all the philosophies of the world, and makes himself the central figure of all history. It is wonderful!"

He half whispered the words, and his eyes had the introspective look of a man who is. thinking deeply.

He came to see me at our cottage on Post street one morning before breakfast. In grading a street, a house in which I had lived and had the ill luck to own, on Pine street, had been undermined, and toppled over into the street below, falling on the slate-roof and breaking all to pieces. He came to tell me of it, and to extend his sympathy.

"I thought I would come first, so you might get the bad news from a friend rather than a stranger. You have lost a house; but it is a small matter. Your little boy there might have put out his eye with a pair of scissors, or he might have swallowed a pin and lost his life. There are many things constantly taking place that are harder to bear than the loss of a house."

Many other wise words did the Rabbi speak, and before he left I felt that a house was indeed a small thing to grieve over.

He spoke with charming freedom and candor of all sorts of people.

"Of Christians, the Unitarians have the best heads, and the Methodists the best hearts. The Roman Catholics hold the masses, because they give their people plenty of form. The masses will never receive truth in its simple essence; they must have it in a way that will make it digestible and assimilable, just as their stomachs demand bread, and meats, and fruits, not their extracts or distilled essences, for daily food. As to Judaism, it is on the eve of great changes. What these changes will be I know not, except that I am sure the God of our fathers will fulfill his promise to Israel. This generation will probably see great things."

"Do you mean the literal restoration of the Jews to Palestine?"

He looked at me with an intense gaze, and hastened not to answer. At last he spoke slowly:

"When the perturbed elements of religious thought crystallize into clearness and enduring forms, the chosen people will be one of the chief factors in reaching that final solution of the problems which convulse this age."

He was one of the speakers at the great Mortara indignation-meeting in San Francisco. The speech of the occasion was that of Colonel Baker, the orator who went to Oregon, and in a single campaign magnetized the Oregonians so completely by his splendid eloquence that, passing by all their old party leaders, they sent him to the United States Senate. No one who heard Baker's peroration that night will ever forget it. His dark eyes blazed, his form dilated, and his voice was like a bugle in battle.

"They tell us that the Jew is accursed of God. This has been the plea of the bloody tyrants and robbers that oppressed and plundered them during the long ages of their exile and agony. But the Almighty God executes his own judgments. Woe to him who presumes to wield his thunderbolts! They fall in blasting, consuming vengeance upon his own head. God deals with his chosen people in judgment; but he says to men, Touch them at your peril! They that spoil them shall be for a spoil; they that carried them away captive shall themselves go into captivity. The Assyrian smote the Jew, and where is the proud Assyrian Empire? Rome ground them under her iron heel, and where is the empire of the Cæsars? Spain smote the Jew, and where is her glory? The desert sands cover the site of Babylon the Great. The power that hurled the hosts of Titus against the holy city Jerusalem was shivered to pieces. The banners of Spain, that floated in triumph over half the world, and fluttered in the breezes of every sea, is now the emblem of a glory that is gone, and the ensign of a power that has waned. The Jews are in the hands of God. He has dealt with them in judgment, but they are still the children of promise. The day of their long exile shall end, and they will return to Zion with songs and everlasting joy upon their heads!"

The words were something like these, but who could picture Baker's oratory? As well try to paint a storm in the tropics. Real thunder and lightning cannot be put on canvas.

The Rabbi made a speech, and it was the speech of a man who had come from his books and prayers. He made a tender appeal for the mother and father of the abducted Jewish boy, and argued the question as calmly, and in as sweet a spirit, as if he had been talking over an abstract question in his study. The· vast crowd looked upon that strange figure with a sort of pleased wonder, and the Rabbi seemed almost unconscious of their presence. He was as free from self-consciousness as a little child, and many a Gentile heart warmed that night to the simple-hearted sage who stood before them pleading for the rights of human nature.

The old man was often very sad. In such moods he would come round to our cottage on Post street, and sit with us until late at night, unburdening his aching heart, and relaxing by degrees into a playfulness that was charming from its very awkwardness. He would bring little picture-books for the children, pat them on their heads, and praise them. They were always glad to see him, and would nestle round him lovingly. We all loved him, and felt glad in the thought that he left our little circle lighter at heart. He lived alone. Once, when I playfully spoke to him of matrimony, he laughed quietly, and said:

"No, no—my books and my poor school-children are enough for me."

He died suddenly and alone. He had been out one windy night visiting the poor, came home sick, and before morning was in that world of spirits which was so real to his faith, and for which he longed. He left his little fortune of a few thousand dollars to the poor of his native village of Posen, in Poland. And thus passed from California-life Dr. Julius Eckman, the Rabbi.

MY MINING SPECULATION.

"I BELIEVE the Lord has put me in the way of making a competency for my old age," said the dear old Doctor, as he seated himself in the arm-chair reserved for him at the cottage at North Beach.

"How?" I asked.

"I met a Texas man to-day, who told me of the discovery of an immensely rich silver mining district in Deep Spring Valley, Mono county, and he says he can get me in as one of the owners."

I laughingly made some remark expressive of incredulity. The honest and benignant face of the old Doctor showed that he was a little nettled.

"I have made full inquiry, and am sure this is no mere speculation. The stock will not be put upon the market, and will not be assessable. They propose to make me a trustee, and the owners, limited in number, will have entire control of the property. But I will not be hasty in the mat-

11 (161)

ter. I will make it a subject of prayer for twenty-four hours, and then if there be no adverse indications I will go on with it."

The next day I met the broad-faced Texan, and was impressed by him as the old Doctor had been.

It seemed a sure thing. An old prospector had been equipped and sent out by a few gentlemen, and he had found outcroppings of silver in a range of hills extending not less than three miles. Assays had been made of the ores, and they were found to be very rich. All the timber and water-power of Deep Spring Valley had been taken up for the company under the general and local pre-emption and mining laws. It was a big thing. The beauty of the whole arrangement was that no "mining sharps" were to be let in; we were to manage it ourselves, and reap all the profits.

We went into it, the old Doctor and I, feeling deeply grateful to the broad-faced Texan, who had so kindly given us the chance. I was made a trustee, and began to have a decidedly business feeling as such. At the meetings of "the board," my opinions were frequently called for, and were given with great gravity. The money was paid for the shares I had taken, and the precious evidences of ownership were carefully put in a place of safety. A mill was built near the richest of the claims, and the assays were good. There were delays, and more money was called for, and sent up. The assays were still good, and the reports from our superintendent were glowing. "The biggest thing in the history of California mining," he wrote; and when the secretary read his letter to the board, there was a happy expression on each face.

At this point I began to be troubled. It seemed, from reasonable ciphering, that I should soon be a millionaire. It made me feel solemn and anxious. I lay awake at night, praying that I might not be spoiled by my good fortune. The scriptures that speak of the deceitfulness of riches were called to mind, and I rejoiced with trembling. Many beneficent enterprises were planned, principally in the line of endowing colleges, and paying church-debts. (I had had an experience in this line.) There were further delays, and more money was called for. The ores were rebellious, and our "process" did not suit them. Fryborg and Deep Spring Valley were not the same. A new superintendent — one that understood rebellious ores — was employed at a higher salary. He reported that all was right, and that we might expect "big news" in a few days, as he proposed to crush about seventy tons of the best rock, "by a new and improved process."

The board held frequent meetings, and in view of the nearness of great results did not hesitate to meet the requisitions made for further outlays of money. They resolved to pursue a prudent but vigorous policy in developing the vast property when the mill should be fairly in operation.

All this time I felt an under-current of anxiety lest I might sustain spiritual loss by my sudden accession to great wealth, and continued to fortify myself with good resolutions.

As a matter of special caution, I sent for a parcel of the ore, and had a private assay made of it. The assay was good.

The new superintendent notified us that on a certain date we might look for a report of the result of the first great crushing and clean-up of the seventy tons of rock. The day came. On Kearny street I met one of the stockholders—a careful Presbyterian brother, who loved money. He had a solemn look, and was walking slowly, as if in deep thought. Lifting his eyes as we met, he saw me, and spoke:

"*It is lead!*"

"What is lead?"

"Our silver mine in Deep Spring Valley."

Yes; from the seventy tons of rock we got eleven dollars in silver, and about fifty pounds of as good lead as was ever molded into bullets.

The board held a meeting the next evening. It was a solemn one. The fifty-pound bar of lead was placed in the midst, and was eyed reproachfully. I resigned my trusteeship, and they saw me not again. That was my first and last mining speculation. It failed somehow—but the assays were all very good.

MIKE REESE.

I HAD business with him, and went at a business hour. No introduction was needed, for he had been my landlord, and no tenant of his ever had reason to complain that he did not get a visit from him, in person or by proxy, at least once a month. He was a punctual man—as a collector of what was due him. Seeing that he was intently engaged, I paused and looked at him. A man of huge frame, with enormous hands and feet, massive head, receding forehead, and heavy cerebral development, full sensual lips, large nose, and peculiar eyes that seemed at the same time to look through you and to shrink from your gaze—he was a man at whom a stranger would stop in the street to get a second gaze. There he sat at his desk, too much absorbed to notice my entrance. Before him lay a large pile of one-thousand-dollar United States Government bonds, and he was clipping off the coupons. That face! it was a study as he sat

(166)

using the big pair of scissors. A hungry boy in the act of taking into his mouth a ripe cherry, a mother gazing down into the face of her pretty sleeping child, a lover looking into the eyes of his charmer, are but faint figures by which to express the intense pleasure he felt in his work. But there was also a feline element in his joy—his handling of those bonds was somewhat like a cat toying with its prey. When at length he raised his head, there was a fierce gleam in his eye and a flush in his face. I had come upon a devotee engaged in worship. This was Mike Reese, the miser and millionaire. Placing his huge left-hand on the pile of bonds, he gruffly returned my salutation,

"Good morning."

He turned as he spoke, and cast a look of scrutiny into my face which said plain enough that he wanted me to make known my business with him at once.

I told him what was wanted. At the request of the official board of the Minna-street Church I had come to ask him to make a contribution toward the payment of its debt.

"O yes; I was expecting you. They all come to me. Father Gallagher, of the Catholic Church, Dr. Wyatt, of the Episcopal Church, and all the others, have been here. I feel friendly to the

Churches, and I treat all alike—it won't do for me to be partial—*I don't give to any!*"

That last clause was an anticlimax, dashing my hopes rudely; but I saw he meant it, and left. I never heard of his departing from the rule of strict impartiality he had laid down for himself.

We met at times at a restaurant on Clay street. He was a hearty feeder, and it was amusing to see how skillfully in the choice of dishes and the thoroughness with which he emptied them he could combine economy with plenty. On several of these occasions, when we chanced to sit at the same table, I proposed to pay for both of us, and he quickly assented, his hard, heavy features lighting up with undisguised pleasure at the suggestion, as he shambled out of the room amid the smiles of the company present, most of whom knew him as a millionaire, and me as a Methodist preacher.

He had one affair of the heart. Cupid played a prank on him that was the occasion of much merriment in the San Francisco newspapers, and of much grief to him. A widow was his enslaver and tormentor—the old story. She sued him for breach of promise of marriage. The trial made great fun for the lawyers, reporters, and the amused public generally; but it was no fun for him. He was mulcted for six thousand dollars and costs of the suit. It was during the time I was renting one of his offices on Washington street. I called to see him, wishing to have some repairs made. His clerk met me in the narrow hall, and there was a mischievous twinkle in his eye as he said:

"You had better come another day—the old man has just paid that judgment in the breach of promise case, and he is in a bad way."

Hearing our voices, he said,

"Who is there?—come in."

I went in, and found him sitting leaning on his desk, the picture of intense wretchedness. He was all unstrung, his jaw fallen, and a most pitiful face met mine as he looked up and said, in a broken voice,

"Come some other day—I can do no business to-day; I am very unwell."

He was indeed sick—sick at heart. I felt sorry for him. Pain always excites my pity, no matter what may be its cause. He was a miser, and the payment of those thousands of dollars was like tearing him asunder. He did not mind the jibes of the newspapers, but the loss of the money was almost killing. He had not set his heart on popularity, but cash.

He had another special trouble, but with a different sort of ending. It was discovered by a neighbor of his that, by some mismeasurement of the surveyors, he (Reese) had built the wall of one of his immense business-houses on Front street six inches beyond his own proper line, taking in just so much of that neighbor's lot. Not being on friendly terms with Reese, his neighbor made a peremptory demand for the removal of the wall, or the payment of a heavy price for the ground. Here was misery for the miser. He writhed in mental agony, and begged for easier terms, but in vain. His neighbor would not relent. The business men of the vicinity rather enjoyed the situation, humorously watching the progress of the affair. It was a case of diamond cut diamond, both parties bearing the reputation of being hard men to deal with. A day was fixed for Reese to give a definite answer to his neighbor's demand, with notice that, in case of his non-compliance, suit against him would be begun at once. The day came, and with it a remarkable change in Reese's tone. He sent a short note to his enemy breathing profanity and defiance.

"What is the matter?" mused the puzzled citizen; "Reese has made some discovery that makes him think he has the upper-hand, else he would not talk this way."

And he sat and thought. The instinct of this class of men where money is involved is like a miracle.

"I have it!" he suddenly exclaimed; "Reese has the same hold on me that I have on him."

Reese happened to be the owner of another lot adjoining that of his enemy, on the other side. It occurred to him that, as all these lots were surveyed at the same time by the same party, it was most likely that as his line had gone six inches too far on the one side his enemy's had gone as much too far on the other. And so it was. He had quietly a survey made of the premises, and he chuckled with inward joy to find that he held this winning card in the unfriendly game. With grim politeness the neighbors exchanged deeds for the two half feet of ground, and their war ended. The moral of this incident is for him who hath wit enough to see it.

For several seasons he came every morning to North Beach to take sea-baths. Sometimes he rode his well-known white horse, but oftener he walked. He bathed in the open sea, making, as one expressed it, twenty-five cents out of the Pacific Ocean, by avoiding the bath-house. Was this the charm that drew him forth so early? It not seldom chanced that we walked down-town together. At times he was quite communicative, speaking of himself in a way that was peculiar. It seems he had thoughts of marrying before his episode with the widow.

"Do you think a young girl of twenty could love an old man like me?" he asked me one day, as we were walking along the street.

I looked at his huge and ungainly bulk, and into his animal face, and made no direct answer. Love! Six millions of dollars is a great sum. Money may buy youth and beauty, but love does not come at its call. God's highest gifts are free; only the second-rate things can be bought with money. Did this sordid old man yearn for pure human love amid his millions? Did such a dream cast a momentary glamour over a life spent in raking among the muck-heaps? If so, it passed away, for he never married.

He understood his own case. He knew in what estimation he was held by the public, and did not conceal his scorn for its opinion.

"My love of money is a disease. My saving and hoarding as I do is irrational, and I know it. It pains me to pay five cents for a street-car ride, or a quarter of a dollar for a dinner. My pleasure in accumulating property is morbid, but I have felt it from the time I was a foot-peddler in Charlotte, Campbell, and Pittsylvania counties, in Virginia, until now. It is a sort of insanity, and it is incurable; but it is about as good a form of madness as any, and all the world is mad in some fashion."

This was the substance of what he said of himself when in one of his moods of free speech, and it gave me a new idea of human nature—a man whose keen and penetrating brain could subject his own consciousness to a cool and correct analysis, seeing clearly the folly which he could not resist. The autobiography of such a man might furnish a curious psychological study, and explain the formation and development in society of those moral monsters called misers. Nowhere in literature has such a character been fully portrayed, though Shakespeare and George Eliot have given vivid touches of some of its features.

He always retained a kind feeling for the South, over whose hills he had borne his peddler's pack when a youth. After the war, two young ex-Confederate soldiers came to San Francisco to seek their fortunes. A small room adjoining my office was vacant, and the brothers requested me to secure it for them as cheap as possible. I applied to Reese, telling him who the young men were, and describing their broken and impecunious condition.

"Tell them to take the room free of rent—but it ought to bring five dollars a month."

It took a mighty effort, and he sighed as he spoke the words. I never heard of his acting similarly in any other case, and I put this down to his credit, glad to know that there was a warm spot in that mountain of mud and ice.   A report of this generous act got afloat in the city, and many were the inquiries I received as to its truth.   There was general incredulity.

His health failed, and he crossed the seas.   Perhaps he wished to visit his native hills in Germany, which he had last seen when a child.   There he died, leaving all his millions to his kindred, save a bequest of one hundred and fifty thousand dollars to the University of California.   What were his last thoughts, what was his final verdict concerning human life, I know not.   Empty-handed he entered the world of spirits, where, the film fallen from his vision, he saw the Eternal Realities. What amazement must have followed his awakening!

UNCLE NOLAN.

HE was black and ugly; but it was an ugliness that did not disgust or repel you. His face had a touch both of the comic and the pathetic. His mouth was very wide, his lips very thick and the color of a ripe damson, blue-black; his nose made up in width what it lacked in elevation; his ears were big, and bent forward; his eyes were a dull white, on a very dark ground; his wool was white and thick. His age might be anywhere along from seventy onward. A black man's age, like that of a horse, becomes dubious after reaching a certain stage.

He came to the class-meeting in the Pine-street Church, in San Francisco, one Sabbath morning. He asked leave to speak, which was granted.

"Bredren, I come here sometime ago, from Vicksburg, Mississippi, where I has lived forty year,. or more. I heered dar was a culud church up on de hill, an' I thought I'd go an' washup wid 'em. I went dar three or fo' Sundays, but I foun' deir ways did n't suit me, an' my ways did n't suit dem. Dey was Yankees' niggers, an' [proudly] I's a Southern man myself. Sumbody tole me dar was a Southern Church down here on Pine street, an' I thought I'd cum an' look in. Soon 's I got inside de church, an' look roun' a minit, I feels at home. Dey look like home-folks; de preacher preach like home-folks; de people sing like home-folks. Yer see, chillun, I 'se a Southern man myself [emphatically], and I 'se a Southern Methodis'. Dis is de Church I was borned in, an' dis is de Church I was *rarred* in, an' [with great energy] dis is de Church which de Scripter says de gates ob hell shall not prevail ag'in it! ["Amen!" from Father Newman and others.] When dey heerd I was comin' to dis Church, some ob 'em got arter me 'bout it. Dey say dis Church was a enemy to de black people, and dat dey was in favor ob slavery. I tole 'em de Scripter said, 'Love your enemies,' an' den I took de Bible an' read what it says about slavery — I can read some, chillun — 'Servants, obey yer masters in all things, not wid eye-service, as men-pleasers, but as unto de Lord;' and so on. But, bless yer souls, chillun, dey would n't lis'en to dat—*so I foun' out dey was abberlishen niggers, an' I lef' 'em !.*"

Yes, he left them, and came to us. I received

him into the Church in due form, and with no little eclat, he being the only son of Ham on our roll of members in San Francisco. He stood firm to his Southern Methodist colors under a great pressure.

"Yer ought ter be killed fer goin' ter dat Southern Church," said one of his colored acquaintances one day, as they met in the street.

"Kill me, den," said Uncle Nolan, with proud humility; "kill me, den; yer can't cheat me out ob many days, nohow."

He made a living, and something over, by rag-picking at North Beach and elsewhere, until the Chinese entered into competition with him, and then it was hard times for Uncle Nolan. His eye-sight partially failed him, and it was pitiful to see him on the beach, his threadbare garments flutter-ing in the wind, groping amid the rubbish for rags, or shuffling along the streets with a huge sack on his back, and his old felt hat tied under his nose with a string, picking his way carefully to spare his swollen feet, which were tied up with bagging and woolens. His religious fervor never cooled; I never heard him complain. He never ceased to be joyously thankful for two things—his freedom and his religion. But, strange as it may seem, he was a pro-slavery man to the last. Even after the war, he stood to his opinion.

12

"Dem niggers in de South thinks dey is free, but dey ain't. 'Fore it's all ober, all dat ain't dead will be glad to git back to deir masters," he would say.

Yet he was very proud of his own freedom, and took the utmost care of his free-papers. He had no desire to resume his former relation to the peculiar and patriarchal institution. He was not the first philosopher who has had one theory for his fellows, and another for himself.

Uncle Nolan would talk of religion by the hour. He never tired of that theme. His faith was simple and strong, but, like most of his race, he had a tinge of superstition. He was a dreamer of dreams, and he believed in them. Here is one which he recited to me. His weird manner, and low, chanting tone, I must leave to the imagination of the reader:

UNCLE NOLAN'S DREAM.

A tall black man came along, an' took me by de arm, an' tole me he had come for me. I said:

"What yer want wid me?"

"I come to carry yer down into de darkness."

"What for?"

"'Cause you did n't follow de Lord."

Wid dat, he pulled me 'long de street till he come to a big black house, de biggest house an' de thickest walls I eber seed. We went in a little

do', an' den he took me down a long sta'rs in de
dark, till we come to a big do'; we went inside,
an' den de big black man locked de do' behin' us.
An' so we kep' on, goin' down, an' goin' down, an'
goin' down, an' he kep' lockin' dem big iron do's
behin' us, an' all de time it was pitch dark, so I
could n't see him, but he still hel' on ter me. At
las' we stopped, an' den he started to go 'way. He
locked de do' behin' him, an' I heerd him goin' up
de steps de way we come, lockin' all de do's behin'
him as he went. I tell you, dat was dreaffle when
I heerd dat big key turn on de outside, an' me 'way
down, down, down dar in de dark all alone, an'
no chance eber to git out! An' I knowed it was
'cause I did n't foller de Lord. I felt roun' de
place, an' dar was nothin' but de thick walls an'
de great iron do'. Den I sot down an' cried,
'cause I knowed I was a los' man. Dat was de
same as hell [his voice sinking into a whisper], an'
all de time I knowed I was dar, 'cause I had n't
follered de Lord. Bymeby somethin' say, "Pray."
Somethin' keep sayin', "Pray." Den I drap on
my knees an' prayed. I tell you, no man eber
prayed harder 'n I did! I prayed, an' prayed, an'
prayed! What's dat? Dar's somebody a-comin'
down dem steps; dey's unlockin' de do'; an' de fus'
thing I knowed, de place was all lighted up bright
as day, an' a white-faced man stood by me, wid a

crown on his head, an' a golden key in his han'. Somehow, I knowed it was Jesus, an' right den I waked up all of a tremble, an' knowed it was a warnin' dat I mus' foller de Lord. An', bless Jesus, I has been follerin' him fifty year since I had dat dream.

In his prayers, and class-meeting and love-feast talks, Uncle Nolan showed a depth of spiritual insight truly wonderful, and the effects of these talks were frequently electrical. Many a time have I seen the Pine-street brethren and sisters rise from their knees, at the close of one of his prayers, melted into tears, or thrilled to religious rapture, by the power of his simple faith, and the vividness of his sanctified imagination.

He held to his pro-slavery views and guarded his own freedom-papers to the last; and when he died, in 1875, the last colored Southern Methodist in California was transferred from the Church militant to the great company that no man can number, gathered out of every nation, and tribe, and kindred, on the earth.

BUFFALO JONES.

THAT is what the boys called him. His real Christian name was Zachariah. The way he got the name he went by was this: He was a Methodist, and prayed in public. He was excitable, and his lungs were of extraordinary power. When fully aroused, his voice sounded, it was said, like the bellowing of a whole herd of buffaloes. It had peculiar reverberations—rumbling, roaring, shaking the very roof of the sanctuary, or echoing among the hills when let out at its utmost strength at a camp-meeting. This is why they called him Buffalo Jones. It was his voice. There never was such another. In Ohio he was a blacksmith and a fighting man. He had whipped every man who would fight him, in a whole tier of counties. He was converted after the old way; that is to say, he was "powerfully" converted. A circuit-rider preached the sermon that converted him. His anguish was awful. The midnight hour found him

(181)

in tears. The Ohio forest resounded with his cries for mercy. When he found peace, it swelled into rapture. He joined the Church militant among the Methodists, and he stuck to them, quarreled with them, and loved them, all his life. He had many troubles, and gave much trouble to many people. The old Adam died hard in the fighting blacksmith. His pastor, his family, his friends, his fellow-members in the Church, all got a portion of his wrath in due season, if they swerved a hair-breadth from the straight-line of duty as he saw it. I was his pastor, and I never had a truer friend, or a severer censor. One Sunday morning he electrified my congregation, at the close of the sermon, by rising in his place and making a personal application of a portion of it to individuals present, and insisting on their immediate expulsion from the Church. He had another side to his character, and at times was as tender as a woman. He acted as class-leader. In his melting moods he moved every eye to tears, as he passed round among the brethren and sisters, weeping, exhorting, and rejoicing. At such times, his great voice softened into a pathos that none could resist, and swept the chords of sympathy with resistless power. But when his other mood was upon him, he was fearful. He scourged the unfaithful with a whip of fire. He would quote with a singular fluency

and aptness every passage of Scripture that blast-
ed hypocrites, reproved the lukewarm, or threatened damnation to the sinner. At such times his
voice sounded like the shout of a warrior in battle,
and the timid and wondering hearers looked as if
they were in the midst of the thunder and lightning of a tropical storm. I remember the shock
he gave a quiet and timid lady whom I had per-
suaded to remain for the class-meeting after service. Fixing his stern and fiery gaze upon her, and
knitting his great bushy eyebrows, he thundered
the question:

"Sister, do you ever pray?"

The startled woman nearly sprang from her seat
in a panic as she stammered hurriedly,

"Yes, sir; yes, sir."

She did not attend his class-meeting again.

At a camp-meeting he was present, and in one
of his bitterest moods. The meeting was not con-
ducted in a way to suit him. He was grim, critical, and contemptuous, making no concealment of
his dissatisfaction. The preaching displeased him
particularly. He groaned, frowned, and in other
ways showed his feelings. At length he could
stand it no longer. A young brother had just
closed a sermon of a mild and persuasive kind,
and no sooner had he taken his seat than the old
man arose. Looking forth upon the vast audience,

and then casting a sharp and scornful glance at the preachers in and around "the stand," he said:

"You preachers of these days have no gospel in you. You remind me of a man going into his barn-yard early in the morning to feed his stock. He has a basket on his arm, and here come the horses nickering, the cows lowing, the calves and sheep bleating, the hogs squealing, the turkeys gobbling, the hens clucking, and the roosters crowing. They all gather round him, expecting to be fed, and lo, his basket is empty! You take texts, and you preach, but you have no gospel. Your baskets are empty."

Here he darted a defiant glance at the astonished preachers, and then, turning to one, he added in a milder and patronizing tone:

"You, Brother Sim, do preach a little gospel—in your basket there is *one little nubbin!*"

Down he sat, leaving the brethren to meditate on what he had said. The silence that followed was deep.

At one time his conscience became troubled about the use of tobacco, and he determined to quit. This was the second great struggle of his life. He was running a saw-mill in the foot-hills at the time, and lodged in a little cabin near by. Suddenly deprived of the stimulant to which it had so long been accustomed, his nervous system was wrought up to a pitch of frenzy. He would rush from the cabin, climb along the hill-side, run leaping from rock to rock, now and then screaming like a maniac. Then he would rush back to the cabin, seize a plug of tobacco, smell it, rub it against his lips, and away he would go again. He smelt, but never tasted it again.

"I was resolved to conquer, and by the grace of God I did," he said.

That was a great victory for the fighting blacksmith.

When a melodeon was introduced into the church, he was sorely grieved and furiously angry. He argued against it, he expostulated, he protested, he threatened, he staid away from church. He wrote me a letter, in which he expressed his feelings thus:

San José, 1860.

DEAR BROTHER:—They have got the devil into the church now! Put your foot on its tail and it squeals.

Z. JONES.

This was his figurative way of putting it. I was told that he had, on a former occasion, dealt with the question in a more summary way, by taking his ax and splitting a melodeon to pieces.

Neutrality in politics was, of course, impossible to such a man. In the civil war his heart was with the South. He gave up when Stonewall Jackson was killed.

"It is all over—the praying man is gone," he said; and he sobbed like a child. From that day he had no hope for the Confederacy, though once or twice, when feeling ran high, he expressed a readiness to use carnal weapons in defense of his political principles. For all his opinions on the subject he found support from the Bible, which he read and studied with unwearying diligence. He took its words literally on all occasions, and the Old Testament history had a wonderful charm for him. He would have been ready to hew any modern Agag in pieces before the Lord.

He finally found his way to the Insane Asylum. The reader has already seen how abnormal was his mind, and will not be surprised that his storm-tossed soul lost its rudder at last. But mid all its veerings he never lost sight of the Star that had shed its light upon his checkered path of life. He raved, and prayed, and wept, by turns. The horrors of mental despair would be followed by gleams of seraphic joy. When one of his stormy moods was upon him, his mighty voice could be heard above all the sounds of that sad and pitiful company of broken and wrecked souls. The old class-meeting instinct and habit showed itself in his semi-lucid intervals. He would go round among the patients questioning them as to their religious feeling and behavior in true class-meeting style. Dr. Shurtleff one day overheard a colloquy between him and Dr. Rogers, a free-thinker and reformer, whose vagaries had culminated in his shaving close one side of his immense whiskers, leaving the other side in all its flowing amplitude. Poor fellow! Pitiable as was his case, he made a ludicrous figure walking the streets of San Francisco half shaved, and defiant of the wonder and ridicule he excited. The ex-class-leader's voice was earnest and loud, as he said:

"Now, Rogers, you must pray. If you will get down at the feet of Jesus, and confess your sins, and ask him to bless you, he will hear you, and give you peace. But if you won't do it," he continued, with growing excitement and kindling anger at the thought, "you are the most infernal rascal that ever lived, and I'll beat you into a jelly!"

The good Doctor had to interfere at this point, for the old man was in the very act of carrying out his threat to punish Rogers bodily, on the bare possibility that he would not pray as he was told to do. And so that extemporized class-meeting came to an abrupt end.

"Pray with me," he said to me the last time I saw him at the Asylum. Closing the door of the little private office, we knelt side by side, and the poor old sufferer, bathed in tears, and docile as a little child, prayed to the once suffering, once crucified, but risen and interceding Jesus. When he arose from his knees his eyes were wet, and his face showed that there was a great calm within. We never met again. He went home to die. The storms that had swept his soul subsided, the light of reason was rekindled, and the light of faith burned brightly; and in a few weeks he died in great peace, and another glad voice joined in the anthems of the blood-washed millions in the city of God.

TOD ROBINSON.

THE image of this man of many moods and brilliant genius that rises most distinctly to my mind is that connected with a little prayer-meeting in the Minna-street Church, San Francisco, one Thursday night. His thin silver locks, his dark flashing eye, his graceful pose, and his musical voice, are before me. His words I have not forgotten, but their electric effect must forever be lost to all except the few who heard them.

"I have been taunted with the reproach that it was only after I was a broken and disappointed man in my worldly hopes and aspirations that I turned to religion. The taunt is just"—here he bowed his head, and paused with deep emotion— "the taunt is just. I bow my head in shame, and take the blow. My earthly hopes have faded and fallen one after another. The prizes that dazzled my imagination have eluded my grasp. I am a broken, gray-haired man, and I bring to my God only the remnant of a life. But, brethren, it is this very thought that fills me with joy and gratitude at this moment—the thought that when all else fails God takes us up. Just when we need him most, and most feel our need of him, he lifts us up out of the depths where we had groveled, and presses us to his Fatherly heart. This is the glory of Christianity. The world turns from us when we fail and fall; then it is that the Lord draws nigher. Such a religion must be from God, for its principles are God-like. It does not require much skill or power to steer a ship into port when her timbers are sound, her masts all rigged, and her crew at their posts; but the pilot that can take an old hulk, rocking on the stormy waves, with its masts torn away, its rigging gone, its planks loose and leaking, and bring it safe to harbor, that is the pilot for me. Brethren, I am that hulk; and Jesus is that Pilot!"

"Glory be to Jesus!" exclaimed Father Newman, as the speaker, with swimming eyes, radiant face, and heaving chest, sunk into his seat. I never heard any thing finer from mortal lips, but it seems cold to me as I read it here. Oratory cannot be put on paper.

He was present once at a camp-meeting, at the famous Toll-gate Camp-ground, in Santa Clara Valley, near the city of San José. It was Sabbath morning, just such a one as seldom dawns on this earth. The brethren and sisters were gathered around "the stand" under the live-oaks for a speaking-meeting. The morning glory was on the summits of the Santa Cruz Mountains that sloped down to the sacred spot, the lovely valley smiled under a sapphire sky, the birds hopped from twig to twig of the overhanging branches that scarcely quivered in the still air, and seemed to peer inquiringly into the faces of the assembled worshipers. The bugle-voice of Bailey led in a holy song, and Simmons led in prayer that touched the eternal throne. One after another, gray-haired men and saintly women told when and how they began the new life far away on the old hills they would never see again, and how they had been led and comforted in their pilgrimage. Young disciples, in the flush of their first love, and the rapture of new-born hope, were borne out on a tide of resistless feeling into that ocean whose waters encircle the universe. The radiance from the heavenly hills was reflected from the consecrated encampment, and the angels of God hovered over the spot. Judge Robinson rose to his feet, and stepped into the altar, the sunlight at that moment falling upon his face. Every voice was hushed, as, with the orator's indefinable magnetism, he drew every eye upon him. The pause was thrilling. At length he spoke:

"This is a mount of transfiguration. The transfiguration is on hill and valley, on tree and shrub, on grass and flower, on earth and sky. It is on your faces that shine like the face of Moses when he came down from the awful mount where he met Jehovah face to face. The same light is on your faces, for here is God's shekinah. This is the gate of heaven. I see its shining hosts, I hear the melody of its songs. The angels of God encamped with us last night, and they linger with us this morning. Tarry with us, ye sinless ones, for this is heaven on earth!"

He paused, with extended arm, gazing upward entranced. The scene that followed beggars description. By a simultaneous impulse all rose to their feet and pressed toward the speaker with awe-struck faces, and when Grandmother Rucker, the matriarch of the valley, with luminous face and uplifted eyes, broke into a shout, it swelled into a melodious hurricane that shook the very hills. He ought to have been a preacher. So he said to me once:

"I felt the impulse and heard the call in my early manhood. I conferred with flesh and blood, and was disobedient to the heavenly vision. I have had some little success at the bar, on the hustings, and in legislative halls, but how paltry has it been in comparison with the true life and high career that might have been mine!"

He was from the hill-country of North Carolina, and its flavor clung to him to the last. He had his gloomy moods, but his heart was fresh as a Blue Ridge breeze in May, and his wit bubbled forth like a mountain-spring. There was no bitterness in his satire. The very victim of his thrust enjoyed the keenness of the stroke, for there was no poison in the weapon. At times he seemed inspired, and you thrilled, melted, and soared, under the touches of this Western Coleridge. He came to my room at the Golden Eagle, in Sacramento City, one night, and left at two o'clock in the morning. He walked the floor and talked, and it was the grandest monologue I ever listened to. One part of it I could not forget. It was with reference to preachers who turn aside from their holy calling to engage in secular pursuits, or in politics.

"It is turning away from angels' food to feed on garbage. Think of spending a whole life in contemplating the grandest things, and working for the most glorious ends, instructing the ignorant, consoling the sorrowing, winning the wayward back to duty and to peace, pointing the dying to Him who is the light and the life of men, animating the living to seek from the highest motives a holy life and a sublime destiny! O it is a life that might draw an angel from the skies! If there is a spe-

13

cial hell for fools, it should be kept for the man who turns aside from a life like this, to trade, or dig the earth, or wrangle in a court of law, or scramble for an office."

He looked at me as he spoke, with flashing eyes and curled lip.

"That is all true and very fine, Judge, but it sounds just a little peculiar as coming from you."

"I am the very man to say it, for I am the man who bitterly sees its truth. Do not make the misstep that I did. A man might well be willing to live on bread and water, and walk the world afoot, for the privilege of giving all his thoughts to the grandest themes, and all his service to the highest objects. As a lawyer, my life has been spent in a prolonged quarrel about money, land, houses, cattle, thieving, slandering, murdering, and other villainy. The little episodes of politics that have given variety to my career have only shown me the baseness of human nature, and the pettiness of human ambition. There are men who will fill these places and do this work, and who want and will choose nothing better. Let them have all the good they can get out of such things. But the minister of the gospel who comes down from the height of his high calling to engage in this scramble does that which makes devils laugh and angels weep."

This was the substance of what he said on this
point. I have never forgotten it. I am glad he
came to my room that night. What else he said
I cannot write, but the remembrance of it is like
to that of a melody that lingers in my soul when
the music has ceased.

"I thank you for your sermon to-day—you never
told a single lie."

This was his remark at the close of a service in
Minna street one Sunday.

"What is the meaning of that remark?"

"That the exaggerations of the pulpit repel
thousands from the truth. Moderation of statement is a rare excellence. A deep spiritual insight enables a religious teacher to shade his mean-
ings where it is required. Deep piety is genius
for the pulpit. Mediocrity in native endowments,
conjoined with spiritual stolidity in the pulpit, does
more harm than all the open apostles of infidelity
combined. They take the divinity out of religion
and kill the faith of those who hear them. None
but inspired men should stand in the pulpit. Religion is not in the intellect merely. The world
by wisdom cannot know God. The attempt to find
out God by the intellect has always been, and always must be, the completest of failures. Religion is the sphere of the supernatural, and stands
not in the wisdom of men, but in the power of

God. It has often happened that men of the first order of talent and the highest culture have been converted by the preaching of men of weak intellect and limited education, but who were directly taught of God, and had drunk deep from the fount of living truth in personal experience of the blessed power of Christian faith. It was through the intellect that the devil seduced the first pair. When we rest in the intellect only, we miss God. With the heart only can man believe unto righteousness. The evidence that satisfies is based on consciousness. Consciousness is the satisfying demonstration.

"Eye hath not seen, nor ear heard, neither have entered into the heart of man, the things which God hath prepared for them that love him. But God hath revealed them unto us by his Spirit. They can be revealed in no other way."

Here was the secret he had learned, and that had brought a new joy and glory into his life as it neared the sunset. The great change dated from a dark and rainy night as he walked home in Sacramento City. Not more tangible to Saul of Tarsus was the vision, or more distinctly audible the voice that spoke to him on the way to Damascus, than was the revelation of Jesus Christ to this lawyer of penetrating intellect, large and varied reading, and sharp perception of human folly and weakness. It was a case of conversion in the fullest and divinest sense. He never fell from the wonder-world of grace to which he had been lifted. His youth seemed to be renewed, and his life had rebloomed, and its winter was turned into spring, under the touch of Him who maketh all things new. He was a new man, and he lived in a new world. He never failed to attend the class-meetings, and in his talks there the flashes of his genius set religious truths in new lights, and the little band of Methodists were treated to bursts of fervid eloquence, such as might kindle the listening thousands of metropolitan churches into admiration, or melt them into tears. On such occasions I could not help regretting anew that the world had lost what this man might have wrought had his path in life taken a different direction at the start. He died suddenly, and when in the city of Los Angeles I read the telegram announcing his death, I felt, mingled with the pain at the loss of a friend, exultation that before there was any reaction in his religious life his mighty soul had found a congenial home amid the supernal glories and sublime joys of the world of spirits. The moral of this man's life will be seen by him for whom this imperfect Sketch has been penciled.

AH LEE.

HE was the sunniest of Mongolians. The Chinaman, under favorable conditions, is not without a sly sense of humor of his peculiar sort; but to American eyes there is nothing very pleasant in his angular and smileless features. The manner of his contact with many Californians is not calculated to evoke mirthfulness. The brick-bat may be a good political argument in the hands of a hoodlum, but it does not make its target play-ful. To the Chinaman in America the situation is new and grave, and he looks sober and holds his peace. Even the funny-looking, be-cued little Chinese children wear a look of solemn inquisitive-ness, as they toddle along the streets of San Fran-cisco by the side of their queer-looking mothers. In his own land, over-populated and misgoverned, the Chinaman has a hard fight for existence. In these United States his advent is regarded some-what in the same spirit as that of the seventeen-

(198)

year locusts, or the cotton-worm. The history of
a people may be read in their physiognomy. The
monotony of Chinese life during these thousands
of years is reflected in the dull, monotonous faces
of Chinamen.

Ah Lee was an exception. His skin was almost
fair, his features almost Caucasian in their regu-
larity; his dark eye lighted up with a peculiar
brightness, and there was a remarkable buoyancy
and glow about him every way. He was about
twenty years old. How long he had been in California I know not. When he came into my office
to see me the first time, he rushed forward and im-
pulsively grasped my hand, saying:

"My name Ah Lee—you Doctor Plitzjellie?"

That was the way my name sounded as he spoke
it. I was glad to see him, and told him so.

"You makee Christian newspaper? You talkee
Jesus? Mr. Taylor tellee me. Me Christian—me
love Jesus."

Yes, Ah Lee was a Christian; there could be no
doubt about that. I have seen many happy converts, but none happier than he. He was not
merely happy—he was ecstatic.

The story of the mighty change was a simple
one, but thrilling. Near Vacaville, the former
seat of the Pacific Methodist College, in Solana
county, lived the Rev. Iry. Taylor, a member of

the Pacific Conference of the Methodist Episcopal Church, South. Mr. Taylor was a praying man, and he had a praying wife. Ah Lee was employed as a domestic in the family. His curiosity was first excited in regard to family prayers. He wanted to know what it all meant. The Taylors explained. The old, old story took hold of Ah Lee. He was put to thinking and then to praying. The idea of the forgiveness of sins filled him with wonder and longing. He hung with breathless interest upon the word of the Lord, opening to him a world of new thought. The tide of feeling bore him on, and at the foot of the cross he found what he sought.

Ah Lee was converted—converted as Paul, as Augustine, as Wesley, were converted. He was born into a new life that was as real to him as his consciousness was real. This psychological change will be understood by some of my readers; others may regard it as they do any other inexplicable phenomenon in that mysterious inner world of the human soul, in which are lived the real lives of us all. In Ah Lee's heathen soul was wrought the gracious wonder that makes joy among the angels of God.

The young Chinese disciple, it is to be feared, got little sympathy outside the Taylor household and a few others. The right-hand of Christian fellowship was withheld by many, or extended in

a cold, half-reluctant way. But it mattered not to
Ah Lee; he had his own heaven. Coldness was
wasted on him. The light within him brightened
every thing without.

Ah Lee became a frequent visitor to our cottage
on the hill. He always came and went rejoicing.
The Gospel of John was his daily study and delight. To his ardent and receptive nature it was
a diamond mine. Two things he wanted to do.
He had a strong desire to translate his favorite
Gospel into Chinese, and to lead his parents to
Christ. When he spoke of his father and mother
his voice would soften, his eyes moisten with tenderness.

"I go back to China and tellee my fader and
mudder allee good news," he said, with beaming
face.

This peculiar development of filial reverence
and affection among the Chinese is a hopeful feature of their national life. It furnishes a solid
basis for a strong Christian nation. The weakening of this sentiment weakens religious susceptibility; its destruction is spiritual death. The
worship of ancestors is idolatry, but it is that form
of it nearest akin to the worship of the Heavenly
Father. The honoring of the father and mother
on earth is the commandment with promise, and it
is the promise of this life and of life everlasting.

There is an interblending of human and divine loves; earth and heaven are unitary in companionship and destiny. The golden ladder rests on the earth and reaches up into the heavens.

About twice a week Ah Lee came to see us at North Beach. These visits subjected our courtesy and tact to a severe test. He loved little children, and at each visit he would bring with him a gaylypainted box filled with Chinese sweetmeats. Such sweetmeats! They were too strong for the palates of even young Californians. What cannot be relished and digested by a healthy California boy must be formidable indeed. Those sweetmeats were—but I give it up, they were indescribable! The boxes were pretty, and, after being emptied of their contents, they were kept.

Ah Lee's joy in his new experience did not abate. Under the touch of the Holy Spirit, his spiritual nature had suddenly blossomed into tropical luxuriance. To look at him made me think of the second chapter of the Acts of the Apostles. If I had had any lingering doubts of the transforming power of the gospel upon all human hearts, this conversion of Ah Lee would have settled the question forever. The bitter feeling against the Chinese that just then found expression in California, through so many channels, did not seem to affect him in the least. He had his Christianity warm from the heart of the Son of God, and no caricature of its features or perversion of its spirit could bewilder him for a moment. He knew whom he had believed. None of these things moved him. O blessed mystery of God's mercy, that turns the night of heathen darkness into day, and makes the desert soul bloom with the flowers of paradise! O cross of the Crucified! Lifted up, it shall draw all men to their Saviour! And O blind and slow of heart to believe! why could we not discern that this young Chinaman's conversion was our Lord's gracious challenge to our faith, and the pledge of success to the Church that will go into all the world with the news of salvation?

Ah Lee has vanished from my observation, but I have a persuasion that is like a burning prophecy that he will be heard from again. To me he types the blessedness of old China new-born in the life of the Lord, and in his luminous face I read the prophecy of the redemption of the millions who have so long bowed before the Great Red Dragon, but who now wait for the coming of the Deliverer.

THE CLIMATE OF CALIFORNIA.

HAD Shakespeare lived in California, he would not have written of the "*winter* of our discontent," but would most probably have found in the summer of that then undiscovered country a more fitting symbol of the troublous times referred to; for, with the fogs, winds, and dust, that accompany the summer, or the "dry season," as it is more appropriately called in California, it is emphatically a season of discontent. In the mountains of the State only are these conditions not found. True, you will find dust even there as the natural consequence of the lack of rain; but that is not, of course, so bad in the mountains; and with no persistent, nagging wind to pick it up and fling it spitefully at you, you soon get not to mind it at all. But of summer in the coast country it is hard to speak tolerantly. The perfect flower of its unloveliness flourishes in San. Francisco, and, more or less hardily, all along the

(204)

coast. From the time the rains cease—generally some time in May—through the six-months' period of their cessation, the programme for the day is, with but few exceptions, unvaried. Fog in the morning—chilling, penetrating fog, which obscures the rays of the morning sun completely, and, dank and "clinging like cerements," swathes every thing with its soft, gray folds. On the bay it hangs, heavy and chill, blotting out every thing but the nearest objects, and at a little distance hardly distinguishable from the water itself. At such times is heard the warning-cry of the fog-horns at Fort Point, Goat Island, and elsewhere—a sound which probably is more like that popularly supposed to be produced by an expiring cow in her last agony than any thing else, but which is not like that or any thing in the world but a fog-horn. The fog of the morning, however, gives way to the wind of the afternoon, which, complete master of the situation by three o'clock P.M., holds stormy sway till sunset. No gentle zephyr this, to softly sway the delicate flower or just lift the fringe on the maiden's brow, but what seamen call a "spanking breeze," that does not hesitate to knock off the hat that is not fastened tightly both fore and aft to the underlying head, or to fling sand and dust into any exposed eye, and which dances around generally among skirts and coat-tails with untiring

energy and persistency.   To venture out on the
streets of San Francisco at such times is really no
trifling matter; and to one not accustomed to it,
or to one of a non-combative disposition, the per-
formance is not a pleasant one.   Still the streets
are always full of hurrying passengers; for, whether
attributable to the extra amount of vitality and
vim that this bracing climate imparts to its children, or to a more direct and obvious cause, the
desire to get in-doors again as soon as possible, the
fact remains the same—that the people of California walk faster than do those of almost any other
country.   Not only men either, who with their
coats buttoned up to their chins, and hats jammed
tightly over their half-shut eyes, present a tolera-
bly secure surface to the attacks of the wind, but
their fairer sisters too can be seen, with their fresh
cheeks and bright eyes protected by jaunty veils,
scudding along in the face or the track of the
wind, as the case may be, with wonderful skill and
grace, looking as trim and secure as to rigging as
the lightest schooner in full sail on their own bay.

   But it is after the sun has gone down from the
cloudless sky, and the sea has recalled its breezes
to slumber for the night, that the fulfillment of the
law of compensation is made evident in this matter.   The nights are of silver, if the days be not
of gold.   And all over the State this blessing of

cool, comfortable nights is spread. At any season, one can draw a pair of blankets over him upon retiring, sure of sound, refreshing slumber, unless assailed by mental or physical troubles to which even this glorious climate of California cannot minister.

The country here during this rainless season does not seem to the Eastern visitor enough like what he has known as country in the summer to warrant any outlay in getting there. He must, however, understand that here people go to the country for precisely opposite reasons to those which influence Eastern tourists to leave the city and betake themselves to rural districts. In the East, one leaves the crowded streets and heated atmosphere of the great city to seek coolness in some sylvan retreat. Here, we leave the chilling winds and fogs of the city to try to get warm where they cannot penetrate. Warm it may be; but the country at this season is not at its best as to looks. The flowers and the grass have disappeared with the rains, the latter, however, keeping in its dry, brown roots, that the sun scorches daily, the germ of all next winter's green. Of the trees, the live-oak alone keeps to the summer livery of Eastern forests. Farther up in the mountain counties, it is very different. No fairer summer could be wished for than that which reigns cloudless here; and with the sparkling champagne of that clear, dry air in his nostrils, our Eastern visitor forgets even to sigh for a summer shower to lay the dreadful dust.   And even in the valleys and around the bay, we must confess that some advantages arise from the no-rain-for-six-months policy. Picnickers can set forth any day, with no fear of the fun of the occasion being wet-blanketed by an unlooked-for shower; and farmers can dispose of their crops according to convenience, often leaving their wheat piled up in the field, with no fear of danger from the elements.

Still we do get very tired of this long, strange summer, and the first rains are eagerly looked for and joyously welcomed.   The fall of the first showers after such a long season of bareness and brownness is almost as immediate in its effects as the waving of a fairy's magic wand over Cinderella, sitting ragged in the ashes and cinders.   The change thus wrought is well described by a poet of the soil in a few picturesque lines:

> Week by week the near hills whitened,
>   In their dusty leather cloaks;
>
> Week by week the far hills darkened,
>   From the fringing plain of oaks;
>
> Till the rains came, and far breaking,
>   On the fierce south-wester tost,
>
> Dashed the whole long coast with color,
>   And then vanished and were lost.

With these rains the grass springs up, the trees put out, and the winds disappear, leaving in the air a wonderful softness. In a month or two the flowers appear, and the hills are covered with a mantle of glory. Bluebells, lupins, buttercups, and hosts of other blossoms, spring up in profusion; and, illuminating every thing, the wild California poppy lifts its flaming torch, typifying well, in its dazzling and glowing color, the brilliant minds and passionate hearts of the people of this land. All these bloom on through the winter, for this is a winter but in name. With no frost, ice, or snow, it is more like an Eastern spring, but for the absence of that feeling of languor and debility which is so often felt in that season. True it-rains a good deal, but by no means constantly, more often in the night; and it is this season of smiles and tears, this winter of flowers and budding trees, in which the glory of the California climate lies. Certainly nothing could be more perfect than a bright winter day in that State. Still, after all I could say in its praise, you would not know its full charm till you had felt its delicious breath on your own brow; for the peculiar freshness and exhilaration of the air are indescribable.

Sometimes in March, the dwellers on the bay are treated to a blow or two from the north, which is about as serious weather as the inhabitant of that

14

favored clime ever experiences. After a night whose sleep has been broken by shrieks of the wind and the rattling of doors and windows, I wake with a dullness of head and sensitiveness of nerve that alone would be sufficient to tell me that the north wind had risen like a thief in the night, and had not, according to the manner of that class, stolen away before morning. On the contrary, he seems to be rushing around with an energy that betokens a day of it. I dress, and look out of my window. The bay is a mass of foaming, tossing waves, which, as they break on the beach just below, cast their spray twenty feet in air. All the little vessels have come into port, and only a few of the largest ships still ride heavily at their anchors. The line separating the shallow water near the shore from the deeper waters beyond is much farther out than usual, and is more distinct. Within its boundary, the predominant white is mixed with a dark, reddish brown; without, the spots of color are darkest green. The sky has been swept of every particle of cloud and moisture, and is almost painfully blue. Against it, Mounts Tamalpais and Diablo stand outlined with startling clearness. The hills and islands round the bay look as cold and uncomfortable in their robes of bright green as a young lady who has put on her spring-dress too soon. The streets and walks are swept bare, but still the air is filled with flying sand that cuts my face like needles, when, later, overcoated and gloved to the utmost, I proceed down-town. Such days are Nature's cleaning days, very necessary to future health and comfort, but, like all cleaning-days, very unpleasant to go through with. With her mightiest besom does the old lady sweep all the cobwebs from the sky, all the dirt and germs of disease from the ground, and remove all specks and impurities from her air - windows. One or two such "northers" finish up the season, effectually scaring away all the clouds, thus clearing the stage for the next act in this annual drama of two acts.

This climate of California is perfectly epitomized in a stanza of the same poem before quoted:

> So each year the season shifted,
>   Wet and warm, and drear and dry,
>
> Half a year of cloud and flowers,
>   Half a year of dust and sky.

AFTER THE STORM.

(Penciled in the bay-window above the Golden Gate, North
Beach, San Francisco, February 20, 1873.)

ALL day the winds the sea had lashed,
The fretted waves in anger dashed
Against the rocks in tumult wild
Above the surges roughly piled—
No blue above, no peace below,
The waves still rage, the winds still blow.

Dull and muffled the sunset gun
Tells that the dreary day is done;
The sea-birds fly with drooping wing—
Chill and shadow on every thing—
No blue above, no peace below,
The waves still rage, the winds still blow.

The clouds dispart; the sapphire dye
In beauty spreads o'er the western sky,
Cloud-fires blaze o'er the Gate of Gold,
Gleaming and glowing, fold on fold—
(212)

All blue above, all peace below,
Nor waves now rage, nor winds now blow.

Souls that are lashed by storms of pain,
Eyes that drip with sorrow's rain;
Hearts that burn with passion strong,
Bruised and torn, and weary of wrong—
No light above, no peace within,
Battling with self, and torn by sin—

Hope on, hold on, the clouds will lift;
God's peace will come as his own sweet gift,
The light will shine at evening-time,
The reflected beams of the sunlit clime,
The blessèd goal of the soul's long quest,
Where storms ne'er beat, and all are blest.

BISHOP KAVANAUGH IN CALIFORNIA.

HE came first in 1856. The Californians "took to" him at once. It was almost as good as a visit to the old home to see and hear this rosy-faced, benignant, and solid Kentuckian. His power and pathos in the pulpit were equaled by his humor and magnetic charm in the social circle. Many consciences were stirred. All hearts were won by him, and he holds them unto this day. We may hope too that many souls were won that will be stars in his crown of rejoicing in the day of Jesus Christ.

At San José, his quality as a preacher was developed by an incident that excited no little popular interest. The (Northern) Methodist Conference was in session at that place, the venerable and saintly Bishop Scott presiding. Bishop Kavanaugh was invited to preach, and it so happened that he was to do so on the night following an appointment for Bishop Scott. The matter was talked

(214)

of in the town, and not unnaturally a spirit of friendly rivalry was excited with regard to the approaching pulpit performances by the Northern and Southern Bishops respectively. One enthusiastic but not pious Kentuckian offered to bet a hundred dollars that Kavanaugh would preach the better sermon. Of course the two venerable men were unconscious of all this, and nothing of the kind was in their hearts. The church was thronged to hear Bishop Scott, and his humility, strong sense, deep earnestness, and holy emotion, made a profound and happy impression on all present. The church was again crowded the next night. Among the audience was a considerable number of Southerners—wild fellows, who were not often seen in such places, among them the enthusiastic Kentuckian already alluded to. Kavanaugh, after going through with the preliminary services, announced his text, and began his discourse. He seemed not to be in a good preaching mood. His wheels drove heavily. Skirmishing around and around, he seemed to be reconnoitering his subject, finding no salient point for attack. The look of eager expectation in the faces of the people gave way to one of puzzled and painful solicitude. The heads of the expectant Southerners drooped a little, and the betting Kentuckian betrayed his feelings by a lowering of the under-jaw and sundry nervous twitchings of the muscles of his face. The good Bishop kept talking, but the wheels revolved slowly. It was a solemn and "trying time" to at least a portion of the audience, as the Bishop, with head bent over the Bible and his broad chest stooped, kept trying to coax a response from that obstinate text. It seemed a lost battle. At last a sudden flash of thought seemed to strike the speaker, irradiating his face and lifting his form as he gave it utterance, with a characteristic throwing back of his shoulders and upward sweep of his arms. Those present will never forget what followed. The afflatus of the true orator had at last fallen upon him; the mighty ship was launched, and swept out to sea under full canvas. Old Kentucky was on her feet that night in San José. It was indescribable. Flashes of spiritual illumination, explosive bursts of eloquent declamation, sparkles of chastened wit, appeals of overwhelming intensity, followed like the thunder and lightning of a Southern storm. The church seemed literally to rock. "Amens" burst from the electrified Methodists of all sorts; these were followed by "halleluiahs" on all sides; and when the sermon ended with a rapturous flight of imagination, half the congregation were on their feet, shaking hands, embracing one another, and shouting. In the tremendous religious impression made, criticism was not thought of. Even the betting Kentuckian showed by his heaving breast and tearful eyes how far he was borne out of the ordinary channels of his thought and feeling.

He came to Sonora, where I was pastor, to preach to the miners. It was our second year in California, and the paternal element in his nature fell on us like a benediction. He preached three noble sermons to full houses in the little church on the red hill-side, but his best discourses were spoken to the young preacher in the tiny parsonage. Catching the fire of the old polemics that led to the battles of the giants in the West, he went over the points of difference between the Arminian and Calvinistic schools of theology in a way that left a permanent deposit in a mind which was just then in its most receptive state. We felt very lonesome after he had left. It was like a touch of home to have him with us then, and in his presence we have had the feeling ever since. What a home will heaven be where all such men will be gathered in one company!

It was a warm day when he went down to take the stage for Mariposa. The vehicle seemed to be already full of passengers, mostly Mexicans and Chinamen. When the portly Bishop presented himself, and essayed to enter, there were frowns and expressions of dissatisfaction.

"Mucho malo!" exclaimed a dark-skinned Señorita, with flashing black eyes.

"Make room in there—he's got to go," ordered the bluff stage-driver, in a peremptory tone.

There were already eight passengers inside, and the top of the coach was covered as thick as robins on a sumac-bush. The Bishop mounted the step and surveyed the situation. The seat assigned him was between two Mexican women, and as he sunk into the apparently insufficient space there was a look of consternation in their faces—and I was not surprised at it. But *scrouging* in, the new-comer smiled, and addressed first one and then another of his fellow-passengers with so much friendly pleasantness of manner that the frowns cleared away from their faces, even the stolid, phlegmatic Chinamen brightening up with the contagious good-humor of the "big Mellican man." When the driver cracked his whip, and the spirited mustangs struck off in the California gallop—the early Californians scorned any slower gait—everybody was smiling. Staging in California in those days was often an exciting business. There were "opposition" lines on most of the thoroughfares, and the driving was furious and reckless in the extreme. Accidents were strangely seldom when we consider the rate of speed, the nature of the roads, and the quantity of bad whisky consumed by most of the drivers. Many of these drivers made it a practice to drink at every stopping-place. Seventeen drinks were counted in one forenoon ride by one of these thirsty Jehus. The racing between the rival stages was exciting enough. Lashing the wiry little horses to full speed, there was but one thought, and that was, to "get in ahead." A driver named White upset his stage between Montezuma and Knight's Ferry on the Stanislaus, breaking his right-leg above the knee. Fortunately none of the passengers were seriously hurt, though some of them were a little bruised and frightened. The stage was righted, White resumed the reins, whipped his horses into a run, and, with his broken limb hanging loose, ran into town ten minutes ahead of his rival, fainting as he was lifted from the seat.

"Old man Holden told me to go in ahead or smash every thing, and I made it!" exclaimed White, with professional pride.

The Bishop was fortunate enough to escape with unbroken bones as he dashed from point to point over the California hills and valleys, though that heavy body of his was mightily shaken up on many occasions.

He came to California on his second visit, in 1863, when the war was raging. An incident occurred that gave him a very emphatic reminder that those were troublous times.

He was at a camp-meeting in the San Joaquin Valley, near Linden—a place famous for gatherings of this sort. The Bishop was to preach at eleven o'clock, and a great crowd was there, full of high expectation. A stranger drove up just before the hour of service—a broad-shouldered man in blue clothes, and wearing a glazed cap. He asked to see Bishop Kavanaugh privately for a few moments.

They retired to "the preachers' tent," and the stranger said:

"My name is Jackson—Colonel Jackson, of the United States Army. I have a disagreeable duty to perform. By order of General McDowell, I am to place you under arrest, and take you to San Francisco."

"Can you wait until I preach my sermon?" asked the Bishop, good-naturedly; "the people expect it, and I don't want to disappoint them if it can be helped."

"How long will it take you?"

"Well, I am a little uncertain when I get started, but I will try not to be too long."

"Very well; go on with your sermon, and if you have no objection I will be one of your hearers."

The secret was known only to the Bishop and his captor. The sermon was one of his best—the vast crowd of people were mightily moved, and the

Colonel's eyes were not dry when it closed. After a prayer, and a song, and a collection, the Bishop stood up again before the people, and said:

"I have just received a message which makes it necessary for me to return to San Francisco immediately. I am sorry that I cannot remain longer, and participate with you in the hallowed enjoyments of the occasion. The blessing of God be with you, my brethren and sisters."

His manner was so bland, and his tone so serene, that nobody had the faintest suspicion as to what it was that called him away so suddenly. When he drove off with the stranger, the popular surmise was that it was a wedding or a funeral that called for such haste. These are two events in human life that admit of no delays: people must be buried, and they will be married.

The Bishop reported to General Mason, Provost-marshal General, and was told to hold himself as in duress until further orders, and to be ready to appear at head-quarters at short notice when called for. He was put on parole, as it were. He came down to San José and stirred my congregation with several of his powerful discourses. In the meantime the arrest had gotten into the newspapers. Nothing that happens escapes the California journalists, and they have even been known to get hold of things that never happened at all. It seems that

some one in the shape of a man had made an affi-
davit that Bishop Kavanaugh had come to the
Pacific Coast as a secret agent of the Southern
Confederacy, to intrigue and recruit in its interest!
Five minutes' inquiry would have satisfied General
McDowell of the silliness of such a charge—but
it was in war times, and he did not stop to make
the inquiry. In Kentucky the good old Bishop
had the freedom of the whole land, coming and
going without hinderance; but the fact was, he had
not been within the Confederate lines since the war
began. To make such an accusation against him
was the climax of absurdity.

About three weeks after the date of his arrest, I
was with the Bishop one morning on our way to
Judge Moore's beautiful country-seat, near San
José, situated on the far-famed Alameda. The
carriage was driven by a black man named Henry.
Passing the post-office, I found, addressed to the
Bishop in my care, a huge document bearing the
official stamp of the provost-marshal's office, San
Francisco. He opened and read it as we drove
slowly along, and as he did so he brightened up,
and turning to Henry, said:

"Henry, were you ever a slave?"

"Yes, sah; in Mizzoory," said Henry, showing
his white teeth.

"Did you ever get your free-papers?"

" Yes, sah—got 'em now."

" Well, I have got mine—let's shake hands."

And the Bishop and Henry had quite a hand-shaking over this mutual experience. Henry enjoyed it greatly, as his frequent chucklings evinced while the Judge's fine bays were trotting along the Alameda.

(I linger on the word Alameda as I write it. It is at least one beneficent trace of the early Jesuit Fathers who founded the San José and Santa Clara missions a hundred years ago. They planted an avenue of willows the entire three miles, and in that rich, moist soil the trees have grown until their trunks are of enormous size, and their branches, overarching the highway with their dense shade, make a drive of unequaled beauty and pleasantness. The horse-cars have now taken away much of its romance, but in the early days it was famous for moonlight drives and their concomitants and consequences. A long-limbed four-year-old California colt gave me a romantic touch of a different sort, nearly the last time I was on the Alameda, by running away with the buggy, and breaking it and me—almost—to pieces. I am reminded of it by the pain in my crippled right-shoulder as I write these lines in July, 1881. But still I say, Blessings on the memory of the Fathers who planted the willows on the Alameda!)

An intimation was given the Bishop that if he wanted the name of the false-swearer who had caused him to be arrested he could have it.

"No, I don't want to know his name," said he; "it will do me no good to know it. May God pardon his sin, as I do most heartily!"

A really strong preacher preaches a great many sermons, each of which the hearers claim to be the greatest sermon of his life. I have heard of at least a half dozen "greatest" sermons by Bascom and Pierce, and other noted pulpit orators. But I heard *one* sermon by Kavanaugh that was probably indeed his master-effort. It had a history. When the Bishop started to Oregon, in 1863, I placed in his hands Bascom's Lectures, which, strange to say, he had never read. Of these Lectures the elder Dr. Bond said "they would be the colossal pillars of Bascom's fame when his printed sermons were forgotten." Those Lectures wonderfully anticipated the changing phases of the materialistic infidelity developed since his day, and applied to them the *reductio ad absurdum* with relentless and resistless power. On his return from Oregon, Kavanaugh met and presided over the Annual Conference at San José. One of his old friends, who was troubled with skeptical thoughts of the materialistic sort, requested him to preach a sermon for his special benefit. This request, and the previous reading of the Lectures, directed his mind to the topic suggested with intense earnestness. The result was, as I shall always think, the sermon of a life-time. The text was, *There is a spirit in man; and the inspiration of the Almighty giveth them understanding.* (Job xxxii. 8.) That mighty discourse was a demonstration of the truth of the affirmation of the text. I will not attempt to reproduce it here, though many of its passages are still vivid in my memory. It tore to shreds the sophistries by which it was sought to sink immortal man to the level of the brutes that perish; it appealed to the consciousness of his hearers in red-hot logic that burned its way to the inmost depths of the coldest and hardest hearts; it scintillated now and then sparkles of wit like the illuminated edges of an advancing thunder-cloud; borne on the wings of his imagination, whose mighty sweep took him beyond the bounds of earth, through whirling worlds and burning suns, he found the culmination of human destiny in the bosom of eternity, infinity, and God. The peroration was indescribable. The rapt audience reeled under it. Inspiration! the man of God was himself its demonstration, for the power of his word was not his own.

"O I thank God that he sent me here this day to hear that sermon! I never heard any thing like it, and I shall never forget it, or cease to be

15

thankful that I heard it," said the Rev. Dr. Charles Wadsworth, of Philadelphia, the great Presbyterian preacher—a man of genius, and a true prose-poet, as any one will concede after reading his published sermons. As he spoke, the tears were in his eyes, the muscles of his face quivering, and his chest heaving with irrepressible emotion. Nobody who heard that discourse will accuse me of too high coloring in this brief description of it.

"Do n't you wish you were a Kentuckian?" was the enthusiastic exclamation of a lady who brought from Kentucky a matchless wit and the culture of Science Hill Academy, which has blessed and brightened so many homes from the Ohio to the Sacramento.

I think the Bishop was present on another occasion when the compliment he received was a left-handed one. It was at the Stone Church in Suisun Valley. The Bishop and a number of the most prominent ministers of the Pacific Conference were present at a Saturday-morning preaching appointment. They had all been engaged in protracted labors, and, beginning with the Bishop, one after another declined to preach. The lot fell at last upon a boyish-looking brother of very small stature, who labored under the double disadvantage of being a very young preacher, and of having been reared in the immediate vicinity. The people were disappointed and indignant when they saw the little fellow go into the pulpit. None showed their displeasure more plainly than Uncle Ben Brown, a somewhat eccentric old brother, who was one of the founders of that Society, and one of its best official members. He sat as usual on a front seat, his thick eyebrows fiercely knit, and his face wearing a heavy frown. He had expected to hear the Bishop, and this was what it had come to! He drew his shoulders sullenly down, and, with his eyes bent upon the floor, nursed his wrath. The little preacher began his sermon, and soon astonished everybody by the energy with which he spoke. As he proceeded, the frown on Uncle Ben's face relaxed a little; at length he lifted his eyes and glanced at the speaker in surprise. He did not think it was in him. With abnormal fluency and force, the little preacher went on with the increasing sympathy of his audience, who were feeling the effects of a generous reaction in his favor. Uncle Ben, touched a little with honest obstinacy as he was, gradually relaxed in the sternness of his looks, straightening up by degrees until he sat upright facing the speaker in a sort of half-reluctant, pleased wonder. Just at the close of a specially vigorous burst of declamation, the old man exclaimed, in a loud voice:

"Bless God! *he uses the weak things of this world*

to confound the mighty!*" casting around a triumph-
ant glance at the Bishop and other preachers.

This impromptu remark was more amusing to
the hearers than helpful to the preacher, I fear;
but it was a way the dear old brother had of speaking out in meeting.

' I must end this Sketch. I have dipped my pen
in my heart in writing it. The subject of it has
been friend, brother, father, to me since the day he
looked in upon us in the little cabin on the hill in
Sonora, in 1855. When I greet him on the hills
of heaven, he will not be sorry to be told that
among the many in the far West to whom he was
helpful was the writer of this too imperfect Sketch.

SANDERS.

H E belonged to the Church militant. In looks
he was a cross between a grenadier and a
Trappist. But there was more soldier than monk
in his nature. He was over six feet high, thin as
a bolster, and straight as a long-leaf pine. His
anatomy was strongly conspicuous. He was the
boniest of men. There were as many angles as
inches in the lines of his face. His hair dis-
dained the persuasions of comb or brush, and
rose in tangled masses above a head that would
have driven a phrenologist mad. It was a long
head in every sense. His features were strong
and stern, his nose one that would have delighted
the great Napoleon — it was a grand organ.
You said at once, on looking at him, Here is a
man that fears neither man nor devil. The face
was an honest face. When you looked into those
keen, dark eyes, and read the lines of that stormy
countenance, you felt that it would be equally

impossible for him to tell a lie or to fear the face of man.

This was John Sanders, one of the early California Methodist preachers. He went among the first to preach the gospel to the gold-hunters. He got a hearing where some failed. His sincerity and brain-power commanded attention, and his pluck enforced respect. In one case it seemed to be needed.

He was sent to preach in Placerville, popularly called in the old days, "Hangtown." It was then a lively and populous place. The mines were rich, and gold-dust was abundant as good behavior was scarce. The one church in the town was a "union church," and it was occupied by Sanders and a preacher of another sect on alternate Sundays. All went well for many months, and if there were no sinners converted in that camp, the few saints were at peace. It so happened that Sanders was called away for a week or two, and on his return he found that a new preacher had been sent to the place, and that he had made an appointment to preach on his (Sanders's) regular day. Having no notion of yielding his rights, Sanders also inserted a notice in the papers of the town that he would preach at the same time and place. The thing was talked about in the town and vicinity, and there was a buzz of excitement. The miners, always ready for a sensation, became interested,

and when Sunday came the church could not hold
the crowd. The strange preacher arrived first, entered the pulpit, knelt a few moments in silent devotion, according to custom, and then sat and surveyed the audience which was surveying him with
curious interest. He was a tall, fine-looking man,
almost the equal of Sanders in height, and superior
to him in weight. He was a Kentuckian originally, but went from Ohio to California, and was a
full-grown man, of the best Western physical type.
In a little while Sanders entered the church, made
his way through the dense crowd, ascended the
pulpit, cast a sharp glance at the intruder, and sat
down. There was a dead silence. The two preachers gazed at the congregation; the congregation
gazed at the preachers. A pin might have been
heard to fall. Sanders was as imperturbable as a
statue, but his lips were pressed together tightly,
and there was a blaze in his eyes. The strange
preacher showed signs of nervousness, moving his
hands and feet, and turning this way and that in
his seat. It was within five minutes of the time for
opening the service. The stranger rose, and was in
the act of taking hold of the Bible that lay on the
cushion in front of him, when Sanders rose to his
full height, stepped in front of him, and darting
lightning from his eyes as he looked him full in
the face, said:

"I preach here to-day, sir!"

That settled it. There was no mistaking that look or tone. The tall stranger muttered an inarticulate protest and subsided. Sanders proceeded with the service, making no allusion to the difficulty until it was ended. Then he proposed a meeting of the citizens the next evening to adjudicate the case. The proposal was acceded to. The church was again crowded; and though ecclesiastically Sanders was in the minority, with the genuine love for fair-play which is a trait of Anglo-Saxon character, he was sustained by an overwhelming majority. It is likely, too, that his plucky bearing the day before made him some votes. A preacher who would fight for his rights suited those wild fellows better than one who would assert a claim that he would not enforce. Sanders preached to larger audiences after this episode in his "Hangtown" pastorate.

It was after this that he went out one day to stake off a lot on which he proposed to build a house of worship. It was near the Roman Catholic Church. A zealous Irishman, who was a little more than half drunk, was standing by. Evidently he did not like any such heretical movements, and, after Sanders had placed the stake in the earth, the Hibernian stepped forward and pulled it up.

"I put the stake back in its place. He pulled it up again. I put it back. He pulled it up again. I put it back once more. He got fiery mad by this time, and started at me with an ax in his hand. I had an ax in my hand, and as its handle was longer than his, *I cut him down.*"

The poor fellow had waked up the fighting preacher, and fell before the sweep of Sanders's ax. He dodged as the weapon descended, and saved his life by doing so. He got an ugly wound on the shoulder, and kept his bed for many weeks. When he rose from his bed he had a profound regard for Sanders, whose grit excited his admiration. There was not a particle of resentment in his generous Irish heart. He became a sober man, and it was afterward a current pleasantry among the "boys" that he was converted by the use of the carnal weapon wielded by that spunky parson. Nobody blamed Sanders for his part in the matter. It was a fair fight, and he had the right on his side. Had he shown the white feather, that would have damaged him with a community in whose estimation courage was the cardinal virtue. Sanders was popular with all classes, and Placerville remembers him to this day. He was no rose-water divine, but thundered the terrors of the law into the ears of those wild fellows with the boldness of a John the Baptist. Many a sinner quaked under

his stern logic and fiery appeals, and some re-
pented.

I shall never forget a sermon he preached at
San José. He was in bad health, and his mind
was morbid and gloomy. His text was, *Who
hath hardened himself against him, and hath pros-
pered?* (Job ix. 4.) The thought that ran through
the discourse was the certainty that retribution
would overtake the guilty. God's law will be up-
held. It protects the righteous, but must crush
the disobedient. He swept away the sophisms
by which men persuade themselves that they can
escape the penalty of violated law; and it seemed
as if we could almost hear the crash of the tum-
bling wrecks of hopes built on false foundations.
God Almighty was visible on the throne of his
power, armed with the seven thunders of his
wrath.

"Who hath defied God and escaped?" he de-
manded, with flashing eyes and trumpet voice.
And then he recited the histories of nations and
men that had made the fatal experiment, and the
doom that had whelmed them in utter ruin.

"And yet you hope to escape!" he thundered
to the silent and awe-struck men and women before him. "You expect that God will abrogate
his law to please you; that he will tear down the
pillars of his moral government that you may be

saved in your sins! O fools, fools, fools! there is no place but hell for such a folly as this!"

His haggard face, the stern solemnity of his voice, the sweep of his long arms, the gleam of his deep-set eyes, and the vigor of his inexorable logic, drove that sermon home to the listeners.

He was the keenest of critics, and often merciless. He was present at a camp-meeting near San José, but too feeble to preach. I was there, and disabled from the effects of the California poison-oak. That deceitful shrub! Its pink leaves smile at you as pleasantly as sin, and, like sin, it leaves its sting. The "preachers' tent" was immediately in the rear of "the stand," and Sanders and I lay inside and listened to the sermons. He was in one of his caustic moods, and his comments were racy enough, though not helpful to devotion.

"There! he yelled, clapped his hands, stamped, and—*said nothing!*"

The criticism was just: the brother in the stand was making a great noise, but there was not much meaning in what he said.

"He made one point only—a pretty good apology for Lazarus's poverty."

This was said at the close of an elaborate discourse on "The Rich Man and Lazarus," by a brother who sometimes got "in the brush."

"He isn't touching his text—he knows no

more theology than a guinea-pig. Words, words, words!"

This last criticism was directed against a timid young divine, who was badly frightened, but who has since shown that there was good metal in him. If he had known what was going on just behind him, he would have collapsed entirely in that tentative effort at preaching the gospel.

Sanders kept up this running fire of criticism at every service, cutting to the bone at every blow, and giving me new light on homiletics, if he did not promote my enjoyment of the preaching. He had read largely and thought deeply, and his incisive intellect had no patience with what was feeble or pointless.

Disease settled upon his lungs, and he rapidly declined. His strong frame grew thinner and thinner, and his mind alternated between moods of morbid bitterness and transient buoyancy. As the end approached, his bitter moods were less frequent, and an unwonted tenderness came into his words and tones. He went to the Lokonoma Springs, in the hills of Napa county, and in their solitudes he adjusted himself to the great change that was drawing near. The capacious blue sky that arched above him, the sighing of the gentle breeze through the solemn pines, the repose of the encircling mountains, bright with sunrise, or purpling in the twilight, distilled the soothing influences of nature into his spirit, and there was a great calm within. *Beyond those California hills the hills of God rose in their supernal beauty before the vision of his faith, and when the summons came for him one midnight, his soul leaped to meet it in a ready and joyous response. On a white marble slab, at the "Stone Church," in Suisun Valley, is this inscription:

REV. JOHN SANDERS.

Many are the afflictions of the righteous, but the Lord delivereth him out of them all.

The spring flowers were blooming on the grave when I saw it last.

A DAY.

AH, that blessed, blessed day! I had gone to the White Sulphur Springs, in Napa County, to get relief from the effects of the California poison-oak. Gay deceiver! With its tender green and pink leaves, it looks as innocent and smiling as sin when it woos youth and ignorance. Like sin, it is found everywhere in that beautiful land. Many antidotes are used, but the only sure way of dealing with it is to keep away from it. Again, there is an analogy: it is easier to keep out of sin than to get out when caught. These soft, pure white sulphur waters work miracles of healing, and attract all sorts of people. The weary and broken-down man of business comes here to sleep, and eat, and rest; the woman of fashion, to dress and flirt; the loudly-dressed and heavily-bejeweled gambler, to ply his trade; happy bridal couples, to have the world to themselves; successful and unsuccessful politicians, to plan future triumphs or brood over

(233)

defeats; pale and trembling invalids, to seek healing or a brief respite from the grave; families es-
caping from the wind and fog of the bay, to spend
a few weeks where they can find sunshine and
quiet—it is a little world in itself. The spot is
every way beautiful, but its chief charm is its iso-
lation. Though within a few hours' ride of San
Francisco, and only two miles from a railroad-sta-
tion, you feel as if you were in the very heart of
nature—and so you are. Winding along the banks
of a sparkling stream, the mountains—great masses
of leafy green—rise abruptly on either hand; the
road bends this way and that until a sudden turn
brings you to a little valley hemmed in all around
by the giant hills. A bold, rocky projection just
above the main hotel gives a touch of ruggedness
and grandeur to the scene. How delicious the feeling of rest that comes over you at once!—the world
shut out, the hills around, and the sky above.

It was in 1863, when the civil war was at its
white heat. Circumstances had given me unde-
sired notoriety in that connection. I had been
thrust into the very vortex of its passion, and my
name made the rallying-cry of opposing elements
in California. The guns of Manassas, Cedar
Mountain, and the Chickahominy, were echoed in
the foot-hills of the Sierras, and in the peaceful
valleys of the far-away Pacific Coast. The good

sense of a practical people prevented any flagrant outbreak on a large scale, but here and there a too ardent Southerner said or did something that gave him a few weeks' or months' duress at Fort Alcatraz, and the honors of a bloodless martyrdom. I was then living at North Beach, in full sight of that fortress. It was kindly suggested by several of my brother editors that it would be a good place for me. When, as my eye swept over the bay in the early morning, the first sight that met my gaze was its rocky ramparts and bristling guns, the poet's line would come to mind: "'T is distance lends enchantment to the view." I was just as close as I wanted to be. "I have good quarters for you," said the brave and courteous Captain McDougall, who was in command at the fort; "and knowing your *penchant*, I will let you have the freedom of a sunny corner of the island for fishing in good weather." The true soldier is sometimes a true gentleman.

The name and image of another Federal officer rise before me as I write. It is that of the heroic soldier, General Wright, who went down with the "Brother Jonathan," on the Oregon coast, in 1865. He was in command of the Department of the Pacific during this stormy period of which I am speaking. I had never seen him, and I had no special desire to make his acquaintance. Somehow Fort Alcatraz had become associated with his name for reasons already intimated. But, though unsought by me, an interview did take place.

"It has come at last!" was my exclamation as I read the note left by an orderly in uniform notifying me that I was expected to report at the quarters of the commanding-general the next day at ten o'clock. Conscious of my innocence of treason or any other crime against the Government or society, my pugnacity was roused by this summons. Before the hour set for my appearance at the military head-quarters, I was ready for martyrdom or any thing else—except Alcatraz. I did n't like that. The island was too small, and too foggy and windy, for my taste. I thought it best to obey the order I had received, and so, punctually at the hour, I repaired to the head-quarters on Washington Street, and ascending the steps with a firm tread and defiant feeling, I entered the room. General Mason, provost-marshal, a scholar and polished gentleman, politely offered me a seat.

"No; I prefer to stand," I said stiffly.

"The General will see you in a few minutes," said he, resuming his work, while I stood nursing my indignation and sense of wrong.

In a little while General Wright entered—a tall and striking figure, silver-haired, blue-eyed, ruddy-

16

faced, with a mixture of the dash of the soldier and the benignity of a bishop.

Declining also his cordial invitation to be seated, I stood and looked at him, still nursing defiance, and getting ready to wear a martyr's crown. The General spoke:

"Did you know, sir, that I am perhaps the most attentive reader of your paper to be found in California?"

"No; I was not aware that I had the honor of numbering the commanding-general of this department among my readers." (This was spoken with severe dignity.)

"A lot of hot-heads have for sometime been urging me to have you arrested on the ground that you are editing and publishing a disloyal newspaper. Not wishing to do any injustice to a fellow-man, I have taken means every week to obtain a copy of your paper, the *Pacific Methodist;* and allow me to say, sir, that no paper has ever come into my family which is such a favorite with all of us."

I bowed, feeling that the spirit of martyrdom was cooling within me. The General continued:

"I have sent for you, sir, that I might say to you, Go on in your present prudent and manly course, and while I command this department you are as safe as I am."

There I stood, a whipped man, my pugnacity all gone, and the martyr's crown away out of my reach. I walked softly down-stairs, after bidding the General an adieu in a manner in marked contrast to that in which I had greeted him at the beginning of the interview. Now that it is all over, and the ocean winds have wailed their dirges for him so many long years, I would pay a humble tribute to the memory of as brave and knightly a man as ever wore epaulettes or fought under the stars and stripes. He was of the type of Sidney Johnston, who fell at Shiloh, and of McPherson, who fell at Kennesaw—all Californians; all Americans, true soldiers, who had a sword for the foe in fair fight in the open field, and a shield for woman, and for the non-combatant, the aged, the defenseless. They fought on different sides to settle forever a quarrel that was bequeathed to their generation, but their fame is the common inheritance of the American people. The reader is beginning to think I am digressing, but he will better understand what is to come after getting this glimpse of those stormy days in the sixties.

The guests at the Springs were about equally divided in their sectional sympathies. The gentlemen were inclined to avoid all exciting discussions, but the ladies kept up a fire of small-arms. When the mails came in, and the latest news was read, comments were made with flashing eyes and flushed cheeks.

The Sabbath morning dawned without a cloud. I awoke with the earliest song of the birds, and was out before the first rays of the sun had touched the mountain-tops. The coolness was delicious, and the air was filled with the sweet odors of aromatic shrubs and flowers, with a hint of the pine-forests and balsam-thickets from the higher altitudes. Taking a breakfast *solus*, pocket-bible in hand I bent my steps up the gorge, often crossing the brook that wound its way among the thickets or sung its song at the foot of the great overhanging cliffs. A shining trout would now and then flash like a silver bar for a moment above the shaded pools. With light step a doe descending the mountain came upon me, and, gazing at me a moment or two with its soft eyes, tripped away. In a narrow pass where the stream rippled over the pebbles between two great walls of rock, a spotted snake crossed my path, hurrying its movement in fright. Fear not, humble ophidian. The war declared between thee and me in the fifteenth verse of the third chapter of Genesis is suspended for this one day. Let no creature die to-day but by the act of God. Here is the lake. How beautiful! how still! A land-slide had dammed the stream where it flowed between steep, lofty banks, backing the waters over a little valley three or four acres in extent, shut in on all sides by the wooded hills, the highest of which rose from its northern margin. Here is my sanctuary, pulpit, choir, and altar. A gigantic pine had fallen into the lake, and its larger branches served to keep the trunk above the water as it lay parallel with the shore. Seated on its trunk, and shaded by some friendly willows that stretch their graceful branches above, the hours pass in a sort of subdued ecstasy of enjoyment. It is peace, the peace of God. No echo of the world's discords reaches me. The only sound I hear is the cooing of a turtle-dove away off in a distant gorge of the mountain. It floats down to me on the Sabbath air with a pathos as if it voiced the pity of Heaven for the sorrows of a world of sin, and pain, and death. The shadows of the pines are reflected in the pellucid depths, and ever and anon the faintest hint of a breeze sighs among their branches overhead. The lake lies without a ripple below, except when from time to time a gleaming trout throws himself out of the water, and, falling with a splash, disturbs the glassy surface, the concentric circles showing where he went down. Sport on, ye shiny denizens of the deep; no angler shall cast his deceitful hook into your quiet haunts this day. Through the foliage of the overhanging boughs the blue sky is spread, a thin, fleecy cloud at times floating slowly along like a watching angel, and casting a momentary shadow upon the watery mirror below. That sky, so deep and so solemn, woos me—lifts my thought till it touches the Eternal. What mysteries of being lie beyond that sapphire sea? What wonders shall burst upon the vision when this mortal shall put on immortality? I open the Book and read. Isaiah's burning song makes new music to my soul attuned. David's harp sounds a sweeter note. The words of Jesus stir to diviner depths. And when I read in the twenty-first chapter of Revelation the Apocalyptic promise of the new heavens and the new earth, and of the New Jerusalem coming down from God out of heaven, a new glory seems to rest upon sky, mountain, forest, and lake, and my soul is flooded with a mighty joy. I am swimming in the Infinite Ocean. Not beyond that vast blue canopy is heaven; it is within my own ravished heart! Thus the hours pass, but I keep no note of their flight, and the evening shadows are on the water before I come back to myself and the world. O hallowed day! O hallowed spot! foretaste and prophecy to the weary and burden-bowed soul of the new heavens and the new earth where its blessed ideal shall be a more blessed reality!

It is nearly dark when I get back to the hotel.

Supper is over, but I am not hungry—I have feasted on the bread of angels.

"Did you know there was quite a quarrel about you this morning?" asks one of the guests.

The words jar. In answer to my look of inquiry, he proceeds:

"There was a dispute about your holding a religious service at the picnic grounds. They made it a political matter—one party threatened to leave if you did preach, the other threatened to leave if you did not preach. There was quite an excitement about it until it was found that you were gone, and then everybody quieted down."

There is a silence. I break it by telling them how I spent the day, and then they are very quiet.

The next Sabbath every soul at the place united in a request for a religious service, the list headed by a high-spirited and brilliant Pennsylvania lady who had led the opposing forces the previous Sunday.

WINTER-BLOSSOMED.

I THINK I saw him the first Sunday I preached in San José, in 1856. He was a notable-looking man. I felt attracted toward him by that indefinable sympathy that draws together two souls born to be friends. I believe in friendship at first sight. Who that ever had a real friend does not? Love at first sight is a different thing—it may be divine and eternal, or it may be a whim or a passing fancy. Passion blurs and blinds in the region of sexual love: friendship is revealed in its own white light.

I was introduced after the service to the stranger who had attracted my attention, and who had given the youthful preacher such a kind and courteous hearing.

"This is Major McCoy."

He was a full head higher than anybody else as he stood in the aisle. He bowed with courtly grace as he took my hand, and his face lighted with a

(248)

smile that had in it something more than a conventional civility. I felt that there was a soul beneath that dignified and courtly exterior. His head displayed great elevation of the cranium, and unusual breadth of forehead. It was what is called an intellectual head; and the lines around the eyes showed the traces of thought, and, as it seemed to me, a tinge of that sadness that nearly always lends its charm to the best faces.

"I have met a man that I know I shall like," was my gratified exclamation to the mistress of the parsonage, as I entered.

And so it turned out. He became one of the select circle to whom I applied the word friend in the sacredest sense. This inner circle can never be large. If you unduly enlarge it you dilute the quality of this wine of life. We are limited. There is only One Heart large enough to hold all humanity in its inmost depths.

My new friend lived out among the sycamores on the New Almaden Road, a mile from the city, and the cottage in which he lived with his cultured and loving household was one of the social paradises of that beautiful valley in which the breezes are always cool, and the flowers never fade.

My friend interested me more and more. He had been a soldier, and in the Mexican war won distinction by his skill and valor. He was with

Joe Lane and his gallant Indianians at Juamant-la, and his name was specially mentioned among those whose fiery onsets had broken the lines of the swarthy foe, and won against such heavy odds the bloody field. He was seldom absent from church on Sunday morning, and now and then his inquiring, thoughtful face would be seen in my smaller audience at night. One unwelcome fact about him pained me, while it deepened my interest in him.

He was a skeptic. Bred to the profession of medicine and surgery, he became bogged in the depths of materialistic doubt. The microscope drew his thoughts downward until he could not see beyond second causes. The soul, the seat of which the scalpel could not find, he feared did not exist. The action of the brain, like that of the heart and lungs, seemed to him to be functional; and when the organ perished did not its function cease forever? He doubted the fact of immortality, but did not deny it. This doubt clouded his life. He wanted to believe. His heart rebelled against the negations of materialism, but his intellect was entangled in its meshes. The Great Question was ever in his thought, and the shadow was ever on his path. He read much on both sides, and was always ready to talk with any from whom he had reason to hope for new light or a helpful suggestion. Did he also pray? We took many long rides and had many long talks together. Pausing under the shade of a tree on the highway, the hours would slip away while we talked of life and death, and weighed the *pros* and *cons* of the mighty hope that we might live again, until the sun would be sinking into the sea behind the Santa Cruz Mountains, whose shadows were creeping over the valley. He believed in a First Cause. The marks of design in Nature left in his mind no room to doubt that there was a Designer.

"The structure and adaptations of the horse harnessed to the buggy in which we sit, exhibit the infinite skill of a Creator."

On this basis I reasoned with him in behalf of all that is precious to Christian faith and hope, trying to show (what I earnestly believe) that, admitting the existence of God, it is illogical to stop short of a belief in revelation and immortality.

> The rudest workman would not fling
>   The fragments of his work away,
>   If every useless bit of clay
> He trod on were a sentient thing.
>
> And does the Wisest Worker take
>   Quick human hearts, instead of stone,
>   And hew and carve them one by one,
> Nor heed the pangs with which they break?

And more: if but creation's waste,
   Would he have given us sense to yearn
   For the perfection none can earn,
And hope the fuller life to taste?

I think, if we must cease to be,
   It is cruelty refined
   To make the instincts of our mind
Stretch out toward eternity.

Wherefore I welcome Nature's cry,
   As earnest of a life again,
   Where thought shall never be in vain,
And doubt before the light shall fly.

My talks with him were helpful to me if not to him. In trying to remove his doubts my own faith was confirmed, and my range of thought enlarged. His reverent spirit left its impress upon mine.

"McCoy is a more religious man than either you or I, Doctor," said Tod Robinson to me one day in reply to a remark in which I had given expression to my solicitude for my doubting friend.

Yes, strange as it may seem, this man who wrestled with doubts that wrung his soul with intense agony, and walked in darkness under the veil of unbelief, had a healthful influence upon me because the attitude of his soul was that of a reverent inquirer, not that of a scoffer.

The admirable little treatise of Bishop McIlvaine, on the "Evidences of Christianity," cleared away some of his difficulties. A sermon of Bishop Kavanaugh, preached at his request, was a help to him. (That wonderful discourse is spoken of elsewhere in this volume.)

A friend of his lay dying at Redwood City. This friend, like himself, was a skeptic, and his doubts darkened his way as he neared the border of the undiscovered country. McCoy went to see him. The sick man, in the freedom of long friendship, opened his mind to him. The arguments of the good Bishop were yet fresh in McCoy's mind, and the echoes of his mighty appeals were still sounding in his heart. Seated by the dying man, he forgot his own misgivings, and with intense earnestness pointed the struggling soul to the Saviour of sinners.

"I did not intend it, but I was impelled by a feeling I could not resist. I was surprised and strangely thrilled at my own words as I unfolded to my friend the proofs of the truth of Christianity, culminating in the incarnation, death, and resurrection, of Jesus Christ. He seemed to have grasped the truths as presented, a great calm came over him, and he died a believer. No incident of my life has given me a purer pleasure than this; but it was a strange thing! Nobody could have had access to him as I had—I, a doubter and a stumbler all my life: it looks like the hand of God!"

His voice was low, and his eyes were wet as he finished the narration.

Yes, the hand of God was in it—it is in every good thing that takes place on earth. By the bed-side of a dying friend, the undercurrent of faith in his warm and noble heart swept away for the time the obstructions that were in his thought, and bore him to the feet of the blessed, pitying Christ, who never breaks a bruised reed. I think he had more light, and felt stronger ever after.

Death twice entered his home-circle—once to convey a budding flower from the earth-home to the skies, and again like a lightning-stroke laying young manhood low in a moment. The instinct within him, stronger than doubt, turned his thought in those dark hours toward God. The ashes of the earthly hopes that had perished in the fire of fierce calamity, and the tears of a grief unspeakable, fertilized and watered the seed of faith which was surely in his heart. The hot furnace-fire did not harden this finely-tempered soul. But still he walked in darkness, doubting, doubting, doubting all he most wished to believe. It was the infirmity of his constitution, and the result of his surround-ings. He went into large business enterprises with mingled success and disappointment. He went into politics, and though he bore himself nobly and gallantly, it need not be said that *that* vortex does not usually draw those who are within its whirl heavenward. He won some of the prizes that were fought for in that arena where the noblest are in danger of being soiled, and where the baser metal sinks surely to the bottom by the inevitable force of moral gravitation.

From time to time we were thrown together, and I was glad to know that the Great Question was still in his thought, and the hunger for truth was still in his heart. Ill health sometimes made him irritable and morbid, but the drift of his inner nature was unchanged. His mind was enveloped in mists, and sometimes tempests of despair raged within him; but his heart still thirsted for the water of life.

A painful and almost fatal railway accident befell him. He was taken to his ranch among the quiet hills of Shasta County. This was the final crisis in his life. Shut out from the world, and shut in with his own thoughts and with God, he reviewed his life and the argument that had so long been going on in his mind. He was now quiet enough to hear distinctly the Still Small Voice whose tones he could only half discern amid the clamors of the world when he was a busy actor on its stage. Nature spoke to him among the hills, and her voice is God's. The great primal instincts of the soul, repressed in the crowd or driven into the background by the mob of petty cares and wants, now had free play in the nature of this man whose soul had so long cried out of the depths for the living God. He prayed the simple prayer of trust at which the gate flies open for the believing soul to enter into the peace of God. He was born into the new life. The flower that had put forth its abortive buds for so many seasons, burst into full bloom at last. With the mighty joy in his heart, and the light of the immortal hope beaming upon him, he passed into the World of Certainties.

A VIRGINIAN IN CALIFORNIA.

"HARD at it, are you, uncle?"

"No, sah—I's workin' by de day, an' I an't a-hurtin' myself."

This answer was given with a jolly laugh as the old man leaned on his pick and looked at me.

"You looked so much like home-folks that I felt like speaking to you. Where are you from?"

"From Virginny, sah!" (pulling himself up to his full height as he spoke). "Where's you from, Massa?"

"I was brought up partly in Virginia too."

"Whar'bouts in Virginny?"

"Mostly in Lynchburg."

"Lynchburg! dat's whar I was fotched up. I belonged to de Widder Tate, dat lived on de New London Road. Gib me yer han', Massa!"

He rushed up to the buggy, and taking my extended hand in his huge fist he shook it heartily, grinning with delight.

17   (257)

This was Uncle Joe, a perfect specimen of the old Virginia "Uncle," who had found his way to California in the early days. Yes, he was a perfect specimen — black as night, his lower limbs crooked, arms long, hands and feet very large. His mouth was his most striking feature. It was the orator's mouth in size, being larger than that of Henry Clay — in fact, it ran almost literally from ear to ear. When he opened it fully, it was like lifting the lid of a box.

Uncle Joe and I became good friends at once. He honored my ministry with his presence on Sundays. There was a touch of dandyism in him that then and there came out. Clad in a blue broadcloth dress-coat of the olden cut, vest to match, tight-fitting pantaloons, stove-pipe hat, and yellow kid gloves, he was a gorgeous object to behold. He knew it, and there was a pleasant self-consciousness in the way he bore himself in the sanctuary.

Uncle Joe was the heartiest laugher I ever knew. He was always as full of happy life as a frisky colt or a plump pig. When he entered a knot of idlers on the streets, it was the signal for a humorous uproar. His quaint sayings, witty repartee, and contagious laughter, never failed. He was as agile as a monkey, and his dancing was a marvel. For a dime he would "cut the pigeonwing," or give a "double-shuffle" or "breakdown" in a way that made the beholder dizzy.

What was Uncle Joe's age nobody could guess—he had passed the line of probable surmising. His own version of the matter on a certain occasion was curious. We had a colored female servant—an old-fashioned aunty from Mississippi—who, with a bandanna handkerchief on her head, went about the house singing the old Methodist choruses so naturally that it gave us a home-feeling to have her about us. Uncle Joe and Aunt Tishy became good friends, and he got into the habit of dropping in at the parsonage on Sunday evenings to escort her to church. On this particular occasion I was in the little study adjoining the dining-room where Aunt Tishy was engaged in cleaning away the dishes after tea. I was not eavesdropping, but could not help hearing what they said. My name was mentioned.

"O yes," said Uncle Joe; "I knowed Massa Fitchjarals back dar in Virginny. I use ter hear 'im preach dar when I was a boy."

There was a silence. Aunt Tishy could n't swallow that. Uncle Joe's statement, if true, would have made me more than a hundred years old, or brought him down to less than forty. The latter was his object; he wanted to impress Aunt Tishy with the idea that he was young enough to be an eligible gallant to any lady. But it failed. That unfortunate remark ruined Uncle Joe's prospects: Aunt Tishy positively refused to go with him to church, and just as soon as he had left she went into the sitting-room in high disgust, saying:

"What made dat nigger tell me a lie like dat? Tut, tut, tut!"

She cut him ever after, saying she would n't keep company with a liar, "even if he was from de Souf." Aunt Tishy was a good woman, and had some old-time notions. As a cook, she was discounted a little by the fact that she used tobacco, and when it got into the gravy it was not improving to its flavor.

Uncle Joe was in his glory at a dinner-party, where he could wait on the guests, give droll answers to the remarks made to call him out, and enliven the feast by his inimitable and "catching" laugh. In a certain circle no occasion of the sort was considered complete without his presence. There was no such thing as dullness when he was about. His peculiar wit or his simplicity was brought out at a dinner-party one day at Dr. Bascom's. There was a large gathering of the leading families of San José and vicinity, and Uncle Joe was there in his jolliest mood. Mrs. Bascom, whose wit was then the quickest and keenest in all California, presided, and enough good things were said to have made a reputation for Sidney Smith or Douglas Jerrold. Mrs. Bascom, herself a Virginian by extraction, had engaged in a laughing colloquy with Uncle Joe, who stood near the head of the table waving a bunch of peacock's feathers to keep off the flies.

"Missus, who is yer kinfolks back dar in Virginny, any way?"

The names of several were mentioned.

"Why, dem's big folks," said Uncle Joe.

"Yes," said she, laughingly; "I belong to the first families of Virginia."

"I do n't know 'bout dat, Missus. I was dar 'fore you was, an' *I* do n't 'long to de fus' families!"

He looked at it from a chronological rather than a genealogical stand-point, and, strange to say, the familiar phrase had never been heard by him before.

Uncle Joe joined the Church. He was sincere in his profession. The proof was found in the fact that he quit dancing. No more "pigeon-wings," "double-shuffles," or "breakdowns," for him—he was a "perfessor." He was often tempted by the offer of coin, but he stood firm.

"No, sah; I's done dancin', an' do n't want to be discommunicated from de Church," he would say, good-naturedly, as he shied off, taking himself away from temptation.

A very high degree of spirituality could hardly be expected from Uncle Joe at that late day; but he was a Christian after a pattern of his own—kind-hearted, grateful, simple-minded, and full of good humor. His strength gradually declined, and he was taken to the county hospital, where his patience and cheerfulness conciliated and elicited kind treatment from everybody. His memories went back to old Virginia, and his hopes looked up to the heaven of which his notions were as simple as those of a little child. In the simplicity of a child's faith he had come to Jesus, and I doubt not was numbered among his little ones. Among the innumerable company that shall be gathered on Mount Zion from every kindred, tribe, and tongue, I hope to meet my humble friend, Uncle Joe.

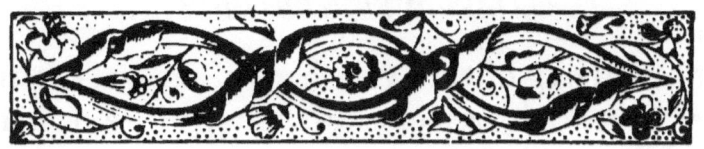

AT THE END.

AMONG my acquaintances at San José, in
1863, was a young Kentuckian who had
come down from the mines in bad health. The
exposure of mining-life had been too severe for
him. It took iron constitutions to stand all day
in almost ice-cold water up to the waist with a hot
sun pouring down its burning rays upon the head
and upper part of the body. Many a poor fellow
sunk under it at once, and after a few days of fever
and delirium was taken to the top of an adjacent
hill and laid to rest by the hands of strangers.
Others, crippled by rheumatic and neuralgic troubles, drifted into the hospitals of San Francisco,
or turned their faces sadly toward the old homes
which they had left with buoyant hopes and elastic
footsteps. Others still, like this young Kentuckian, came down into the valleys with the hacking
cough and hectic flush to make a vain struggle
against the destroyer that had fastened upon their

vitals, nursing often a vain hope of recovery to the very last. Ah, remorseless flatterer! as I write these lines, the images of your victims crowd before my vision: the strong men that grew weak, and pale, and thin, but fought to the last inch for life; the noble youths who were blighted just as they began to bloom; the beautiful maidens etherealized into almost more than mortal beauty by the breath of the death-angel, as autumn leaves, touched by the breath of winter, blush with the beauty of decay. My young friend indulged no false hopes. He knew he was doomed to early death, and did not shrink from the thought. One day, as we were conversing in a store up-town, he said:

"I know that I have at most but a few months to live, and I want to spend them in making preparation to die. You will oblige me by advising me what books to read. I want to get clear views of what I am to do, and then do it."

It need scarcely be said that I most readily complied with his request, and that first and chiefly I advised him to consult the Bible, as the light to his path and the lamp to his feet. Other books were suggested, and a word with regard to prayerful reading was given, and kindly received.

One day I went over to see my friend. Entering his room, I found him sitting by the fire with a table by his side, on which was lying a Bible. There was an unusual flush in his face, and his eye burned with unusual brightness.

"How are you to-day?" I asked.

"I am annoyed, sir—I am indignant," he said.

"What is the matter?"

"Mr. ——, the —— preacher, has just left me. He told me that my soul cannot be saved unless I perform two miracles: I must, he said, think of nothing but religion, and be baptized by immersion. I am very weak, and cannot fully control my mental action—my thoughts will wander in spite of myself. As to being put under the water, that would be immediate death; it would bring on a hemorrhage of the lungs, and kill me."

He leaned his head on the table and panted for breath, his thin chest heaving. I answered:

"Mr. —— is a good man, but narrow. He meant kindly in the foolish words he spoke to you. No man, sick or well, can so control the action of his mind as to force his thoughts wholly into one channel. I cannot do it, neither can any other man. God requires no such absurdity of you or anybody else. As to being immersed, that seems to be a physical impossibility, and he surely does not demand what is impossible. My friend, it really makes little difference what Mr. —— says, or what I say, concerning this matter. What does God say? Let us see."

I took up the Bible, and he turned a face upon me expressing the most eager interest. The blessed Book seemed to open of itself to the very words that were wanted. "Like as a father pitieth his children, so the Lord pitieth them that fear him." "He knoweth our frame, and remembereth that we are dust." "Ho, every one that thirsteth, come to the waters."

Glancing at him as I read, I was struck with the intensity of his look as he drank in every word. A traveler dying of thirst in the desert could not clutch a cup of cold water more eagerly than he grasped these tender words of the pitying Father in heaven.

I read the words of Jesus: "Come unto me all ye that labor and are heavy-laden, and I will give you rest." "Him that cometh unto me I will in no wise cast out."

"This is what God says to you, and these are the only conditions of acceptance. Nothing is said about any thing but the desire of your heart and the purpose of your soul. O my friend, these words are for *you!*"

The great truth flashed upon his mind, and flooded it with light. He bent his head and wept. We knelt and prayed together, and when we rose from our knees he said softly, as the tears stole down his face:

"It is all right now—I see it clearly; I see it clearly!"

We quietly clasped hands, and sat in silent sympathy. There was no need for any words from me; God had spoken, and that was enough. Our hearts were singing together the song without words.

"You have found peace at the cross—let nothing disturb it," I said, as he pressed my hand at the door as we left.

It never was disturbed. The days that had dragged so wearily and anxiously during the long, long months, were now full of brightness. A subdued joy shone in his face, and his voice was low and tender as he spoke of the blessed change that had passed upon him. The Book whose words had been light and life to him was often in his hand, or lay open on the little table in his room. He never lost his hold upon the great truth he had grasped, nor abated in the fullness of his joy. I was with him the night he died. He knew the end was at hand, and the thought filled him with solemn joy. His eyes kindled, and his wasted features fairly blazed with rapture as he said, holding my hand with both of his:

"I am glad it will all soon be over. My peace has been unbroken since that morning when God sent you to me. I feel a strange, solemn joy at the thought that I shall soon know all."

Before day-break the great mystery was disclosed to him, and as he lay in his coffin next day, the smile that lingered on his lips suggested the thought that he had caught a hint of the secret while yet in the body.

Among the casual hearers that now and then dropped in to hear a sermon in Sonora, in the early days of my ministry there, was a man who interested me particularly. He was at that time editing one of the papers of the town, which sparkled with the flashes of his versatile genius. He was a true Bohemian, who had seen many countries, and knew life in almost all its phases. He had written a book of adventure which found many readers and admirers. An avowed skeptic, he was yet respectful in his allusions to sacred things, and I am sure his editorial notices of the pulpit efforts of a certain young preacher who had much to learn were more than just. He was a brilliant talker, with a vein of enthusiasm that was very delightful. His spirit was generous and frank, and I never heard from his lips an unkind word concerning any human being. Even his partisan editorials were free from the least tinge of asperity —and this is a supreme test of a sweet and courte-

ous nature. In our talks he studiously evaded the
one subject most interesting to me. With gentle
and delicate skill he parried all my attempts to
introduce the subject of religion in our conversa-
tions.

"I can't agree with you on that subject, and we
will let it pass," he would say, with a smile, and
then he would start some other topic, and rattle on
delightfully in his easy, rapid way.

He could not stay long at a place, being a confirmed wanderer. He left Sonora, and I lost sight
of him. Retaining a very kindly feeling for this
gentle-spirited and pleasant adventurer, I was loth
thus to lose all trace of him. Meeting a friend one
day, on J Street, in the city of Sacramento, he said:

"Your old friend D—— is at the Golden Eagle
hotel. You ought to go and see him."

I went at once. Ascending to the third story, I
found his room, and, knocking at the door, a feeble
voice bade me enter. I was shocked at the spectacle that met my gaze. Propped in an arm-chair
in the middle of the room, wasted to a skeleton,
and of a ghastly pallor, sat the unhappy man.
His eyes gleamed with an unnatural brightness,
and his features wore a look of intense suffering.

"You have come too late, sir," he said, before I
had time to say a word. "You can do me no good
now. I have been sitting in this chair three weeks.

I could not live a minute in any other position. Hell could not be worse than the tortures I have suffered! I thank you for coming to see me, but you can do me no good—none, none!"

He paused, panting for breath; and then he continued, in a soliloquizing way:

"I played the fool, making a joke of what was no joking matter. It is too late. I can neither think nor pray, if praying would do any good. I can only suffer, suffer, suffer!"

The painful interview soon ended. To every cheerful or hopeful suggestion which I made he gave but the one reply:

"Too late!"

The unspeakable anguish of his look, as his eyes followed me to the door, haunted me for many a day, and the echo of his words, "Too late!" lingered sadly upon my ear. When I saw the announcement of his death, a few days afterward, I asked myself the solemn question, Whether I had dealt faithfully with this light-hearted, gifted man when he was within my reach. His last look is before me now, as I pencil these lines.

"John A—— is dying over on the Portrero, and his family wants you to go over and see him."

It was while I was pastor in San Francisco. A—— was a member of my Church, and lived on

what was called the Portrero, in the southern part
of the city, beyond the Long Bridge. It was after
night when I reached the little cottage on the slope
above the bay.

"He is dying and delirious," said a member of
the family, as I entered the room where the sick
man lay. His wife, a woman of peculiar traits
and great religious fervor, and a large number of
children and grandchildren, were gathered in the
dying man's chamber and the adjoining rooms.
The sick man—a man of large and powerful frame
—was restlessly tossing and moving his limbs, mut-
tering incoherent words, with now and then a burst
of uncanny laughter. When shaken, he would
open his eyes for an instant, make some meaning-
less ejaculation, and then they would close again.
The wife was very anxious that he should have a
lucid interval while I was there.

"O I cannot bear to have him die without a
word of farewell and comfort!" she said, weeping.

The hours wore on, and the dying man's pulse
showed that he was sinking steadily. Still he lay
unconscious, moaning and gibbering, tossing from
side to side as far as his failing strength permitted.
His wife would stand and gaze at him a few moments, and then walk the floor in agony.

"He can't last much longer," said a visitor, who
felt his pulse and found it almost gone, while his

breathing became more labored. We waited in silence. A thought seemed to strike the wife. Without saying a word, she climbed upon the bed, took her dying husband's head upon her lap, and, bending close above his face, began to sing. It was a melody I had never heard before—low, and sweet, and quaint. The effect was weird and thrilling as the notes fell tremulous from the singer's lips in the hush of that dead hour of the night. Presently the dying man became more quiet, and before the song was finished he opened his eyes as a smile swept over his face, and as his glance fell on me I saw that he knew me. He called my name, and looked up in the face that bent above his own, and kissed it.

"Thank God!" his wife exclaimed, her hot tears falling on his face, that wore a look of strange serenity. Then she half whispered to me, her face beaming with a softened light:

"That old song was one we used to sing together when we were first married in Baltimore."

On the stream of music and memory he had floated back to consciousness, called by the love whose instinct is deeper and truer than all the science and philosophy in the world.

At dawn he died, his mind clear, and the voice of prayer in his ears, and a look of rapture in his face.

Dan W——, whom I had known in the mines in the early days, had come to San José about the time my pastorate in the place began. He kept a meat-market, and was a most genial, accommodating, and good-natured fellow. Everybody liked him, and he seemed to like everybody. His animal spirits were unfailing, and his face never revealed the least trace of worry or care. He "took things easy," and never quarreled with his luck. Such men are always popular, and Dan was a general favorite, as the generous and honest fellow deserved to be. Hearing that he was very sick, I went to see him. I found him very low, but he greeted me with a smile.

"How are you to-day, Dan?" I asked, in the off-hand way of the old times.

"It is all up with me, I guess," he replied, pausing to get breath between the words; "the doctor says I can't get out of this—I must leave in a day or two."

He spoke in a matter-of-fact way, indicating that he intended to take death, as he had taken life, easy.

"How do you feel about changing worlds, my old friend?"

"I have no say in the matter. *I have got to go, and that is all there is of it.*"

That was all I ever got out of him. He told me he had not been to church for ten years, as "it

18

was not in his line." He did not understand matters of that sort, he said, as his business was running a meat-market. He intended no disrespect
to me or to sacred things—this was his way of putting the matter in his simple-heartedness.

"Shall I kneel here and pray with you?" I
asked.

"No; you need n't take the trouble, parson," he
said, gently; "you see I 've got to go, and that 's
all there is of it. I do n't understand that sort of
thing—it 's not in my line, you see. I 've been in
the meat business."

"Excuse me, my old friend, if I ask if you do
not, as a dying man, have some thoughts about
God and eternity?"

"That 's not in my line, and I could n't do much
thinking now any way. It 's all right, parson—I 've
got to go, and Old Master will do right about it."

Thus he died without a prayer, and without a
fear, and his case is left to the theologians who can
understand it, and to the "Old Master" who will
do right.

I was called to see a lady who was dying at
North Beach, San Francisco. Her history was a
singularly sad one, illustrating the ups and downs
of California life in a startling manner. From
opulence to poverty, and from poverty to sorrow,

and from sorrow to death—these were the acts in the drama, and the curtain was about to fall on the last. On a previous visit I had pointed the poor sufferer to the Lamb of God, and prayed at her bedside, leaving her calm and tearful. Her only daughter, a sweet, fresh girl of eighteen, had two years ago betrothed herself to a young man from Oregon, who had come to San Francisco to study a profession. The dying mother had expressed a desire to see them married before her death, and I had been sent for to perform the ceremony.

"She is unconscious, poor thing!" said a lady who was in attendance, "and she will fail of her dearest wish."

The dying mother lay with a flushed face, breathing painfully, with closed eyes, and moaning piteously. Suddenly her eyes opened, and she glanced inquiringly around the room. They understood her. The daughter and her betrothed were sent for. The mother's face brightened as they entered, and she turned to me and said, in a faint voice:

"Go on with the ceremony, or it will be too late for me. God bless you, darling!" she added as the daughter bent down sobbing, and kissed her.

The bridal couple kneeled together by the bed of death, and the assembled friends stood around in solemn silence, while the beautiful formula of the

Church was repeated, the dying mother's eyes resting upon the kneeling daughter with an expression of unutterable tenderness. When the vows were taken that made them one, and their hands were clasped in token of plighted faith, she drew them both to her in a long embrace, and then almost instantly closed her eyes with a look of infinite restfulness, and never opened them again.

Of the notable men I met in the mines in the early days, there was one who piqued and puzzled my curiosity. He had the face of a saint with the habits of a debauchee. His pale and student-like features were of the most classic mold, and their expression singularly winning, save when at times a cynical sneer would suddenly flash over them like a cloud-shadow over a quiet landscape. He was a lawyer, and stood at the head of the bar. He was an orator whose silver voice and magnetic qualities often kindled the largest audiences into the wildest enthusiasm. Nature had denied him no gift of body or mind requisite to success in life; but there was a fatal weakness in his moral constitution. He was an inveterate gambler, his large professional earnings going into the coffers of the faro and monte dealers. His violations of good morals in other respects were flagrant. He worked hard by day, and gave himself up to his vices at night. Public opinion was not very exacting in those days, and his failings were condoned by a people who respected force and pluck, and made no close inquiries into a man's private life, because it would have been no easy thing to find one who, on the score of innocence, was entitled to cast the first stone. Thus he lived from year to year, increasing his reputation as a lawyer of marked ability, and as a politician whose eloquence in every campaign was a tower of strength to his party. His fame spread until it filled the State, and his money still fed his vices. He never drank, and that cool, keen intellect never lost its balance, or failed him in any encounter on the hustings or at the bar. I often met him in public, but he never was known to go inside a church. Once, when in a street conversation I casually made some reference to religion, a look of displeasure passed over his face, and he abruptly left me. I was agreeably surprised when, on more than one occasion, he sent me a substantial token of good-will, but I was never able to analyze the motive that prompted him to do so. This remembrance softens the feelings with which these lines are penciled. He went to San Francisco, but there was no change in his life.

"It is the old story," said an acquaintance of whom I made inquiry concerning him: "he has a large and lucrative practice, and the gamblers get all he makes. He is getting gray, and he is failing a little. He is a strange being."

It happened afterward that his office and mine were in the same building and on the same floor. As we met on the stairs, he would nod to me and pass on. I noticed that he was indeed "failing." He looked weary and sad, and the cold or defiant gleam in his steel-gray eyes was changed into a wistful and painful expression that was very pathetic. I did not dare to invade his reserve with any tender of sympathy. Joyless and hopeless as he might be, I felt instinctively that he would play out his drama alone. Perhaps this was a mistake on my part: he may have been hungry for the word I did not speak. God knows. I was not lacking in proper interest in his well-being, but I have since thought in such cases it is safest to speak.

"What has become of B——?" said my landlord one day as we met in the hall. "I have been here to see him several times, and found his door locked, and his letters and newspapers have not been touched. There is something the matter, I fear."

Instantly I felt somehow that there was a tragedy in the air, and I had a strange feeling of awe as I passed the door of B——'s room.

A policeman was brought, the lock forced, and we went in. A sickening odor of chloroform filled the room. The sight that met our gaze made us shudder. Across the bed was lying the form of a man partly dressed, his head thrown back, his eyes staring upward, his limbs hanging loosely over the bedside.

"Is he dead?" was asked in a whisper.

"No," said the officer, with his finger on B——'s wrist; "he is not dead yet, but he will never wake out of this. He has been lying thus two or three days."

A physician was sent for, and all possible efforts made to rouse him, but in vain. About sunset the pulse ceased to beat, and it was only a lump of lifeless clay that lay there so still and stark. This was his death—the mystery of his life went back beyond my knowledge of him, and will only be known at the judgment-day.

One of the gayest and brightest of all the young people gathered at a May-day picnic, just across the bay from San Francisco, was Ada D——. The only daughter of a wealthy citizen, living in one of the lovely valleys beyond the coast-range of mountains, beautiful in person and sunny in temper, she was a favorite in all the circle of her associations. Though a petted child of fortune, she was not spoiled. Envy itself was changed into affection in the presence of a spirit so gentle, unassuming, and loving. She had recently been graduated from one of the best schools, and her graces of character matched the brilliance of her pecuniary fortune.

A few days after the May-day festival, as I was sitting in my office, a little before sunset, there was a knock at the door, and before I could answer the messenger entered hastily, saying:

"I want you to go with me at once to Amador Valley. Ada D—— is dying, and wishes to be baptized. We just have time for the six o'clock boat to take us across the bay, where the carriage and horses are waiting for us. The distance is thirty miles, and we must run a race against death."

We started at once: no minister of Jesus Christ hesitates to obey a summons like that. We reached the boat while the last taps of the last bell were being given, and were soon at the landing on the opposite side of the bay. Springing ashore, we entered the vehicle which was in readiness. Grasping the reins, my companion touched up the spirited team, and we struck across the valley. My driver was an old Californian, skilled in all horsecraft and road-craft. He spoke no word, putting his soul and body into his work, determined, as he had said, to make the thirty miles by nine o'clock. There was no abatement of speed after we struck the hills: what was lost in going up was regained in going down. The mettle of those California-bred horses was wonderful; the quick beating of their hoofs upon the graveled road was as regular as the motion of machinery, steam-driven. It was an exciting ride, and there was a weirdness in the sound of the night-breeze floating by us, and ghostly shapes seemed looking at us from above and below, as we wound our way through the hills, while the bright stars shone like funeral-tapers over a world of death. Death! how vivid and awful was its reality to me as I looked up at those shining worlds on high, and then upon the earth wrapped in darkness below! Death! his sable coursers are swift, and we may be too late! The driver shared my thoughts, and lashed the panting horses to yet greater speed. My pulses beat rapidly as I counted the moments.

"Here we are!" he exclaimed, as we dashed down the hill and brought up at the gate. "It is eight minutes to nine," he added, glancing at his watch by the light of a lamp shining through the window.

"She is alive, but speechless, and going fast," said the father, in a broken voice, as I entered the house.

He led me to the chamber of the dying girl. The seal of death was upon her. I bent above her, and a look of recognition came into her eyes. Not a moment was to be lost.

"If you know me, my child, and can enter the meaning of what I say, indicate the fact if you can."

There was a faint smile and a slight but significant inclination of the fair head as it lay enveloped with its wealth of chestnut curls. With her hands folded on her breast, and her eyes turned upward, the dying girl lay in listening attitude, while in a few words I explained the meaning of the sacred rite and pointed her to the Lamb of God as the one sacrifice for sin. The family stood round the bed in awed and tearful silence. As the crystal sacramental drops fell upon her brow a smile flashed quickly over the pale face, there was a slight movement of the head—and she was gone! The upward look continued, and the smile never left the fair, sweet face. We fell upon our knees, and the prayer that followed was not for her, but for the bleeding hearts around the couch where she lay smiling in death.

Dave Douglass was one of that circle of Tennesseans who took prominent parts in the early history of California. He belonged to the Sumner County Douglasses, of Tennessee, and had the family warmth of heart, impulsiveness, and courage, that nothing could daunt. In all the political contests of the early days he took an active part, and was regarded as an unflinching and unselfish partisan by his own party, and as an open-hearted and generous antagonist by the other. He was elected Secretary of State, and served the people with fidelity and efficiency. He was a man of a powerful physical frame, deep-chested, ruddy-faced, blue-eyed, with just enough shagginess of eyebrows and heaviness of the under-jaw to indicate the indomitable pluck which was so strong an element in his character. He was a true Douglass, as brave and true as any of the name that ever wore the kilt or swung a claymore in the land of Bruce. His was a famous Methodist family in Tennessee, and though he knew more of politics than piety, he was a good friend to the Church, and had regular preaching in the school-house near his farm on the Calaveras River. All the itinerants that traveled that circuit knew "Douglass's School-house" as an appointment, and shared liberally in the hospitality and purse of the General—(that was his title).

"Never give up the fight!" he said to me, with flashing eye, the last time I met him in Stockton, pressing my hand with a warm clasp. It was while I was engaged in the effort to build a church in that place, and I had been telling him of the difficulties I had met in the work. That word and hand-clasp helped me.

He was taken sick soon after. The disease had taken too strong a grasp upon him to be broken. He fought bravely a losing battle for several days. Sunday morning came, a bright, balmy day. It was in the early summer. The cloudless sky was deep-blue, the sunbeams sparkled on the bosom of the Calaveras, the birds were singing in the trees, and the perfume of the flowers filled the air and floated in through the open window to where the strong man lay dying. He had been affected with the delirium of fever during most of his sickness, but that was past, and he was facing death with an unclouded mind.

"I think I am dying," he said, half inquiringly.

"Yes—is there any thing we can do for you?"

His eyes closed for a few moments, and his lips moved as if in mental prayer. Opening his eyes, he said:

"Sing one of the old camp-meeting songs."

A preacher present struck up the hymn, "Show pity, Lord, O Lord forgive."

The dying man, composed to rest, lay with folded hands and listened with shortening breath and a rapt face, and thus he died, the words and the melody that had touched his boyish heart among the far-off hills of Tennessee being the last sounds that fell upon his dying ear. We may hope that on that old camp-meeting song was wafted the prayer and trust of a penitent soul receiving the kingdom of heaven as a little child.

During my pastorate at Santa Rosa, one of my occasional hearers was John I——. He was deputy-sheriff of Sonoma County, and was noted for his quiet and determined courage. He was a man of few words, but the most reckless desperado knew that he could not be trifled with. When there was an arrest to be made that involved special peril, this reticent, low-voiced man was usually intrusted with the undertaking. He was of the good old Primitive Baptist stock from Caswell County, North Carolina, and had a lingering fondness for the peculiar views of that people. He had a weakness for strong drink that gave him trouble at times, but nobody doubted his integrity any more than they doubted his courage. His wife was an earnest Methodist, one of a family of sisters remarkable for their excellent sense and strong religious characters. Meeting him one day, just before my return to San Francisco, he said, with a warmth of manner not common with him:

"I am sorry you are going to leave Santa Rosa.

You understand me, and if anybody can do me any good, you are the man."

There was a tremor in his voice as he spoke, and he held my hand in a lingering grasp.

Yes, I knew him. I had seen him at church on more than one occasion with compressed lips struggling to conceal the strong emotion he felt, sometimes hastily wiping away an unbidden tear. The preacher, when his own soul is aglow and his sympathies all awakened and drawn out toward his hearers, is almost clairvoyant at times in his perception of their inner thoughts. I understood this man, though no disclosure had been made to me in words. I read his eye, and marked the wishful and anxious look that came over his face when his conscience was touched and his heart moved. Yes, I knew him, for my sympathy had made me responsive, and his words, spoken sadly, thrilled me, and rolled upon my spirit the burden of a soul. IIis health, which had been broken by hardships and careless living, began to decline more rapidly. I heard that he had expressed a desire to see me, and made no delay in going to see him. I found him in bed, and much wasted.

"I am glad you have come. I have been wanting to see you," he said, taking my hand. "I have been thinking of my duty to God for a good while, and have felt more than anybody has suspected.

I want to do what I can and ought to do. You have made this matter a study, and you ought to understand it. I want you to help me."

We had many interviews, and I did what I could to guide a penitent sinner to the sinner's Friend. He was indeed a penitent sinner—shut out from the world and shut in with God, the merciful Father was speaking to his soul, and all its depths were stirred. The patient, praying wife had a wishful look in her eyes as I came out of his room, and I knew her thought. God was leading him, and he was receptive of the truth that saves. He had one difficulty.

"I hate meanness, or any thing that looks like it. It does look mean for me to turn to religion now that I am sick, after being so neglectful and wicked when I was well."

"That thought is natural to a manly soul, but there is a snare in it. You are thinking what others may say, and your pride is touched. You are dealing with God only. Ask only what will please him. The time for a man to do his duty is when he sees it and feels the obligation. Let the past go—you cannot undo it, but it may be forgiven. The present and an eternal future are yours, my friend. Do what will please God, and all will be right."

The still waters were reached, and his soul lay at rest in the arms of God. O sweet, sweet rest!

infinitely sweet to the spirit long tossed upon the stormy sea of sin and remorse. O peace of God, the inflow into a human heart of the very life of the Lord! It is the hidden mystery of love divine whispered to the listening ear of faith. It had come to him by its own law when he was ready to receive it. The great change had come to him—it looked out from his eyes and beamed from his face.

He was baptized at night. The family had gathered in the room. . In the solemn hush of the occasion the whispers of the night-breeze could be heard among the vines and flowers outside, and the rippling of the sparkling waters of Santa Rosa Creek was audible. The sick man's face was luminous with the light that was from within. The solemn rite was finished, a tender and holy awe filled the room; it was the house of God and the gate of heaven. The wife, who was sitting near a window, rose, and noiselessly stepped to the bed, and without a word printed a kiss on her husband's forehead, while the joy that flushed her features told that the prayer of thirty years had been answered. We sung a hymn and parted with tears of silent joy. In a little while he crossed the river where we may mingle our voices again by and by. There is not money enough in the California hills to buy the memory of that visit to Santa Rosa.

www.ingramcontent.com/pod-product-compliance
Lightning Source LLC
Chambersburg PA
CBHW020900020726
47497CB00005B/1498